The Last Marilyn Monroe

A Novel

Sonia Hu

Long Publishing Corp.

SONIA HU

Sonia Hu is a writer whose works have been featured in Chinese publications in China, Taiwan, and the United States. Her biographical book *Shanghai Forever Lost* and her nonfiction collection *Reminiscence of Fleeting Time* earned the Excellent Creative Award for Overseas Chinese Film and Television Literature in 2022 and the Top Prize at the Overseas Chinese Literary Awards in 2023. In November 2024, her debut short documentary, *From Stone to Stone*, won the Best Director award at the Berlin Independent Film Festival. She resides in upstate New York with her husband, artist Stone Chun Shi, whose work has inspired her writing.

Long Publishing Corp.

The Last Marilyn Monroe CONTENT

LOVE IS A CHOICE

The Last Marilyn Monroe

The Last Marilyn Monroe is a fictional novella inspired by factual artwork. Centered around a unique oil painting, it tells a heartfelt story of finding love and meaning in life.

Lisha, a Chinese investment adviser living in New York, is a devoted art enthusiast. Struck by the beauty and uniqueness of a larger-than-life oil painting, she devises a bold plan with the help of her family and friends to "sneak" the painting into a museum for the public to appreciate. Unexpectedly, the painting gains widespread acclaim, putting their reputations and careers at risk. The group had to undertake another daring mission—to "sneak" the painting from the museum.

Set against the vibrant backdrop of New York City, The Last Marilyn Monroe explores the intricate emotional entanglements and aspirations of its characters. As the story unfolds, the secrets behind the painting come to light: Why did a master artist choose resolution after finding his own visual language? How did a group of friends with cultural race and ethnicity diversity rediscover the meaning of love and life through a "mission impossible"?

Encounter is fate, but love is a choice. Life is filled with challenges and uncertainty, but by choosing love, we find the courage to walk through the darkest valley to embrace the light of our souls.

The Metropolitan Museum of Art

The Metropolitan Museum of Art lay shrouded in silence on a tranquil New York evening. Heavy footsteps echoed through the hallowed halls as several shadowy figures carefully maneuvered a bulky object. Suddenly, the piercing wail of an alarm shattered the stillness, reverberating through the museum's vast spaces. The deafening sound startled the group carrying a large painting, leaving them paralyzed.

Their faces were shrouded in shadow in the dim light, but they were startled by the blaring alarm, momentarily frozen in uncertainty.

"Damn it!" Jonathan muttered. As a museum staff member, his instincts kicked in, and he instinctively loosened his grip on the painting, causing it to jolt downward. The sudden weight shift nearly toppled the person next to him.

"What the hell!" came the angry retort. Under the faint glow, the speaker's face was revealed: James, assistant director of the Department of Contemporary Art Administration at the Metropolitan Museum.

"Someone must have tripped the infrared sensors!" another voice hissed in a low tone. Panic rippled through the group as they exchanged anxious glances. What had seemed like a flawless plan now unraveled before their eyes. Their faces, filled with dread, mirrored the realization that they were caught red-handed in a scheme gone wrong.

Among them, James, the mastermind behind this audacious operation, felt the most profound tension—not for himself, but for the friends he had drawn into this. His trusted companions now found themselves branded as art thieves, implicated in an act that could have lifelong consequences. Guilt churned in his chest as he silently berated himself for putting them in this precarious position.

At that moment, James longed for a cloak of invisibility to shield them from the unfolding disaster—or perhaps the powers of an extraterrestrial capable of transporting them all to the far reaches of Mars—anything to escape the spiraling chaos.

As the alarm's shrill tones reverberated, James felt his mind slipping into a whirlwind of anxious thoughts, the cacophony morphing into a dissonant, cinematic soundtrack. He was transported back in time to a version of himself from mere months ago: a by-the-book professional, rigidly adhering to the rules, fiercely protective of his coveted position at the Metropolitan Museum, a job he had once believed defined his identity and success.

Chapter I. **The First Encounter**

A Thought–provoking Masterpiece

At the opening of an art exhibition in a spacious gallery converted from an old factory in Brooklyn, New York, Lisha wandered casually among the throngs of guests, glancing at the oil paintings displayed on the walls. This independent, nonprofit gallery was one of the many spaces in Brooklyn offering a platform for innovative contemporary artists curated by independent art organizers.

Lisha, a woman in her mid-thirties, exuded the sleek professionalism of Wall Street in a black dress, carrying an elegant but brandless black handbag. The only pop of color that hinted at her personality was a bright scarf inspired by a Van Gogh painting draped around her neck.

As she strolled, a large painting on one wall suddenly caught her wandering gaze.

Lisha stared at the painting before her as if she could not move her feet. It was an oil portrait of Marilyn Monroe, larger than life, smiling enigmatically as if meeting the viewer's gaze.

Through the crowd, the sight of Lisha standing motionless before the towering portrait, gazing intently, created a striking image. Mailyn Monroe's mysterious and evocative smile bore an uncanny resemblance to the Mona Lisa. As the camera panned toward Mailyn Monroe face, the vibrant colors of the portrait began to break down into distinct square-shaped cubes of oil paint—a kaleidoscope of textures and hues resembling a surreal ocean of color.

It was no ordinary painting. Up close, the composition revealed intricate, raised cubes of color with edges resembling the delicate strokes of Chinese calligraphy. The cubes seemed to ripple endlessly, flowing seamlessly into one another. Yet, as one stepped back, the abstract cubes resolved into the vivid, unmistakable likeness of Marilyn Monroe. Her glamorous long lashes, half-closed eyes, and radiant red lips, accompanied by a faint, indescribable melancholy in her smile, created the illusion that she was alive, standing before Lisha and silently confiding her inner turmoil.

Lisha was captivated. At that moment, a memory from her past resurfaced—a distant image of her late grandmother, Aliza, from an old hand-colored photo taken at the Sam Sanzetti Studio in Shanghai during the 1940s. The photograph depicted young Aliza posing gracefully as a ballerina, her youthful beauty enhanced by her half-Russian Jewish heritage. Her eyes sparkled with vitality, and a similar enigmatic smile graced her lips.

5

Aliza had passed away many years ago, and her photograph had become a faint relic of Lisha's childhood memories. But now, the Marilyn Monroe's portrait vividly conjured those memories, enveloping Lisha in indescribable emotions. It felt like the echoes of time had converged, overwhelming her thoughts with a cascade of recollections.

"Lisha," a deep male voice called from behind her. Lisha's boyfriend, James Smith, approached, balancing two glasses of red wine. He handed one to her and remarked, "This gallery has a good vibe, but the wine? Total party wine."

In his mid-thirties, James had sandy brown hair and a penchant for black attire—a black T-shirt, trousers, and a black Apple Watch adorning his wrist. Yet, as he handed her the glass, he noticed her transfixed by the painting, seemingly oblivious to his remark.

Following her gaze, James turned to the painting and was momentarily taken aback. "Wow," he exclaimed. "I can't believe a nonprofit gallery has something this striking. It's incredible!"

Still gazing at the painting, Lisha remarked, "Don't you think this oil painting is grand? It's so much better than Andy Warhol's Marilyn Monroe!" I love it. I'm buying it."

James was startled, "That thing's huge! Do you even have space for it in your apartment?"

"I'll make space," Lisha replied confidently, "There's a large wall near the balcony in my living room. It'll fit."

After the exhibition, Lisha and James strolled arm in arm to a nearby Japanese restaurant. Under the dim glow of the bar's neon lights, James wrapped an arm around her as though to kiss her, but Lisha tilted her head back slightly and asked, "What do you think of that painting?"

James, slightly bemused, replied, "It's unforgettable, that's for sure."

"I've decided to buy it," Lisha said with a determined smile.

James suggested earnestly, "You don't know anything about the artist or the background of this painting. If you really want to buy it, you should learn about its history from the gallery first."

"Have you ever felt an instant connection or love at first sight?" Lisha asked.

James hesitated, then shook his head slightly, "The moment I saw you for the first time, I knew I liked you. That spark, that feeling—if that's what love at first sight is, then yes, I've felt it."

Lisha laughed, "Oh, poor James, you can't even be sure if your soul has ever come alive!"

James was left speechless. After dating Lisha for over a year, he still couldn't fully understand what this clever, enigmatic woman was constantly thinking.

Love At First Sight

James first met Lisha in the exhibition halls of the Metropolitan Museum of Art in Manhattan, where he worked. At the time, he was hurrying through the Impressionist gallery when a poised and elegant

Asian woman stopped him to ask for directions to *the Companions in Solitude: Reclusion and Communion in Chinese Art.*.

When James first saw Lisha, his eyes lit up, struck by a peculiar sense of familiarity—a feeling he rarely experienced when meeting women. He paused in his tracks and, turning back to look at her, stole a glance to take in her appearance. She stood out from the other Asian women he often encountered in Manhattan. She wasn't clad in designer outfits or carrying an expensive handbag. Instead, she had a black art-themed canvas tote issued by the museum slung casually over one shoulder. Her relaxed attire included comfortable leisurewear and a pair of black Nike sneakers.

Lisha wore light makeup, eschewing bright lipstick or dramatic false eyelashes, and her manner of speaking was warm and composed. James, who had dated a few Asian women before, was familiar with the assertive demeanor often stereotyped as "dragon lady." But Lisha seemed nothing like that. She exuded an understated elegance and a calm demeanor, speaking with a soft-spoken politeness. Her English carried the subtle cadence of a local New Yorker, so polished that without careful attention, one wouldn't detect the accent of a non-native speaker.

"I'll take you there," James offered. "My office is nearby." In truth, his office wasn't in that direction—he just wanted to spend more time with her.

Lisha said, feeling embarrassed. "I assumed you were a gallery attendant. That's why I asked. You don't have to guide me. If you just point me in the right direction, I can find it."

"It's no trouble," James said with a friendly smile. "It's not every day a beautiful woman asks me for directions!" The words had barely left his mouth when he realized how awkward they sounded. It came across as a cheesy pickup line, though his intentions were genuine— he simply wanted to express how rare it was to meet someone who intrigued him.

Lisha frowned slightly and said, "Do you always chat up women like this?"

James stammered, "No, not at all. I'm usually busy with work and rarely come to the galleries. I hardly talk to anyone, let alone a beautiful woman." He quickly added, "Sorry, I didn't mean to offend you. It's just that I feel like I've met you before."

Lisha laughed warmly, "Haha, you mean we're destined to meet? That's what we Chinese would call Yuanfen—a bond brought by fate. It sounds poetic in Chinese, but translating it into English sounds corny."

James relaxed, chuckling along. As they walked together, Lisha's conversation intrigued him. She seemed effortlessly intelligent, and her words carried a subtle depth.

Since meeting Lisha, James has started reading books about spirituality, philosophy, and psychology—all titles she had recommended. Over time, He found himself slowly falling in love with this sometimes enigmatic woman, wanting to see her every day and dreading each time they had to part.

That first spring after meeting Lisha, James invited her to Central

Park. Sitting on a bench under the blooming cherry blossoms, they watched the petals drift gently to the ground.

"I've fallen in love with you," James confessed, breaking the silence.

Lisha turned to him, her bright eyes shimmering. James thought he could see the reflection of cherry blossoms in her gaze. He leaned in and kissed her softly. Lisha neither reciprocated nor pulled away but remained calm, accepting the sudden gesture.

James felt slightly awkward and didn't know what to say next.

Lisha looked at him thoughtfully and said, "I like you very much, but..."

The word "but" hit James like a jolt. His face revealed a hint of disappointment.

Lisha continued, "But love is a heavy word. It comes with a profound sense of responsibility. If you feel the responsibility, please don't say love lightly."

James misunderstood what she meant and was taken aback. "Are you talking about marriage?" he asked.

Lisha shook her head, "Marriage is just a formality. Love itself is a deeply significant feeling that compels you to give everything for it. Too many people are fixated on marriage without truly understanding love. Love encompasses so much—family, history, even destiny. Let me tell you a story about my grandmother, Aliza ."

Tales of Old Shanghai

Lisha's grandmother, Aliza, came from a Russian Jewish family that fled to Shanghai during the Bolshevik Revolution. The Bolshevik Revolution had swept through Russia like a storm, forcing her family to leave their homeland and embark on a journey fraught with uncertainty and hardship. In the 1920s, the family trekked from Siberia to Northeast China, eventually settling in Harbin for a while. Harbin, a thriving multicultural city, became a haven for many Jewish refugees fleeing Russia. However, the volatile political landscape soon pushed them further south, leading them to choose Shanghai as their final destination.

At that time, Shanghai was an international metropolis, offering refuge to immigrants and exiles from around the world. Aliza's family joined a community of over 20,000 Russian émigrés in the city, a quarter of whom were Jewish. They established their community within the vibrant and diverse urban environment, creating a rich social and cultural ecosystem. Towering synagogues graced the skyline, Jewish newspapers circulated widely, and hospitals and charities supported those in need. Despite the distance from their homeland, they preserved their traditions and faith, building a hopeful "second homeland" in Shanghai.

Aliza was born in Shanghai in 1930. Her father, a Russian Jewish physician, was the chief doctor at a Jewish missionary hospital, while her mother, a Shanghai native, was the head nurse at the same institution. The family lived in the French Concession, a cosmopolitan enclave that seamlessly blended cultural traditions with modernity.

Growing up in the French Concession, Aliza was surrounded by a unique blend of tradition and international influences. Her parents strongly emphasized education, ensuring that Aliza received a solid academic foundation despite the family's turbulent history. She was enrolled in a French lycée, one of the most prestigious schools in Shanghai at the time, known for its rigorous curriculum and vibrant artistic atmosphere. Here, Aliza first encountered Western classical art, sparking her deep passion for painting.

Aliza's favorite pastime was strolling through Shanghai's charming streets and alleyways with her sketchbook and pencils, capturing the city's everyday life. From the bustling commercial hubs along the Bund to the tranquil tree-lined avenues of the French Concession, she meticulously recorded it all: the lively street vendors, the dappled sunlight on shikumen courtyards, and the rickshaw pullers passing by. For Aliza, sketching was her way of forging an intimate connection with the city.

Her artistic talent didn't go unnoticed in school. Aliza's art teacher frequently praised her unique perspective and keen eye for detail, and her classmates often gathered around her easel, marveling at her depictions of Shanghai's vibrant street scenes. Her works reflected a profound affection for the city and a remarkable ability to capture life's subtleties. Through art, Aliza found a creative outlet and a source of spiritual fulfillment.

Upon graduating high school, Aliza had a stunning portrait taken at Sam Sanzetti's photography studio on Route Cardinal Mercier (Maoming South Road), owned by a Jewish photographer. The portrait was so captivating that it was displayed in the studio's showcase for an extended period. The photograph caught the eye of Mr. Mo, a student at St. John's University in Shanghai, who was utterly mesmerized by her beauty. Mr. Mo inquired about Aliza's address from the studio and sent her an English letter inviting her and a friend to attend the university's Christmas dance.

At the Christmas dance, Aliza was captivated by the dashing and graceful Mr. Mo, whose charm and elegant dancing swept her off her feet. She found herself falling in love for the first time. Keeping their relationship a secret from their parents, the two embarked on a year-long romance, often strolling through the streets and alleys of Shanghai's concessions. Together, they watched movies, shared popsicles, danced at the Paramount Ballroom, and left traces of love across the city.

Aliza's parents, however, disapproved of the relationship. They hoped their daughter would marry a Jewish boy and leave Shanghai with the family when the time came. But Aliza, deeply in love, was undeterred. To her mother, she retorted, "Didn't you marry a Jewish man despite your parents' objections?"

Eventually, her mother persuaded Aliza's father, pointing out that Mr. Mo came from a well-off Shanghai family and planned to pursue further studies in the United States. Convinced by his prospects, her father reluctantly gave his blessing.

In the summer of 1949, Aliza and Mr. Mo were married in a grand ceremony in Shanghai. They planned to leave for America in the fall, but their plans were disrupted when Aliza discovered she was pregnant. They decided to delay their departure.

That summer, the political landscape in Shanghai shifted dramatically. The Communist Party defeated the Nationalists and took control of the city. Aliza, deeply immersed in her pregnancy, paid little attention to the outside world. But tragedy struck when her baby died shortly after birth, plunging her into grief. By the time she began to recover, Shanghai had changed irrevocably.

Many missionary schools and hospitals were shut down, and foreign staff withdrew from Shanghai. Aliza's parents and extended family prepared to emigrate, urging her and Mr. Mo to join them. However, Mr. Mo, now teaching at a university in Shanghai, was reluctant to leave his family and job. Torn between love and familial duty, Alizachose stays with her husband.

In 1952, Aliza's parents, brothers, and relatives left for the United States. Before their departure, her mother pleaded with Mr. Mo to continue applying to American universities so the family could reunite one day. However, diplomatic relations between China and the U.S. were severed shortly after, and the borders closed. Aliza and Mr. Mo found themselves trapped in a Shanghai that no longer resembled the carefree city of her youth.

While the iconic buildings along the Bund still stood, the city's spirit had been reshaped by new political campaigns and the Soviet-inspired governance system. Despite these upheavals, Aliza persevered. After graduating, she enrolled in a teacher's college and began teaching at a local high school. In 1958, the birth of her first daughter, Mo Hua, marked a turning point. She abandoned lingering thoughts about leaving China and dedicated herself to raising her children.

In 1967, her second daughter, Molly, was born. Aliza and Mr. Mo managed to maintain a modest, quiet life amidst the turbulence of the Cultural Revolution, carefully navigating the political storms.

A devastating blow struck Mr. Mo in 1969. At the end of that year, unable to endure the torment of the political movements, Mr. Mo, who held a professorship at the university, took his own life. It left Aliza and her two daughters to depend on each other for survival. Mr. Mo's passing became a profound, lifelong sorrow for Aliza, plunging her into a period of unbearable anguish.

When China reinstated its college entrance exams in 1977, Mo Hua seized the opportunity to change her destiny. She was admitted to a prestigious university in Beijing, where she excelled. Later, she married a visual artist from the Central Academy of Fine Arts. The family's fortunes began to shift as China entered its era of reform and opening up in the 1980s.

During this time, Aliza, who was fluent in French, resumed her teaching career as a French instructor. By the early 1990s, when Mo Hua gave birth to Lisha, she traveled to Beijing to help care for her granddaughter. She poured all her love into raising Lisha, becoming a steadfast figure in the child's life.

It was then that Aliza learned from her brothers, who had returned from the United States to visit, that their parents had both passed away. Before their deaths, they had constantly spoken of her, their only wish being to see their beloved daughter one last time in this life.

Aliza listened, tears streaming down her face, and decided not to go to America. Initially, she had planned to go with Mr. Mo, but now that both he and her parents were gone, she was all alone. Shanghai had become her home.

Before Lisha left for her studies in America, Aliza embraced her tightly and said, "You're still young, and you can choose your own path. Remember, love is a choice and a responsibility. Never forget to cherish the people who matter most to you. My greatest regret is that I couldn't fulfill my filial duties to my parents." Her voice trembled slightly as though weighed down by deep remorse and regret. "Back then, I chose to stay—not because I didn't love them, but because Mr. Mo needed me. Yet sometimes, making a choice means letting go and accepting the consequences of that sacrifice.

Lisha hugged her grandmother and promised, "Don't worry, Grandma. I'll only marry for love—or not at all."

It was the last time Lisha saw Aliza alive. A few years later, Aliza passed away suddenly. At the time, Lisha was in the critical phase of transitioning from a work visa to a green card, unable to return to China to attend the funeral. She could only mourn her grandmother silently from across the ocean, the regret of not being able to say goodbye leaving a hidden wound that deepened with time. Aliza's smile, her voice, and their shared memories often resurfaced in the quiet of the night, transforming into an ache that lingered in Lisha's heart.

This longing gradually evolved into an obsession with uncovering Aliza's past, like a thread entwined with her soul, pulling her toward revisiting her grandmother's story. Yet, each recollection seemed to deepen an invisible void, as if an unresolved farewell and an unspoken closure were like a silent undertow, perpetually churning within her. Her soul remained restless, as though awaiting a way to complete the goodbye that had never been.

The arrival of *The Last Marilyn Monroe* felt like a warm ray of light piercing through the shadows of Lisha's deeply buried sorrow, dispelling the loneliness and confusion that had lingered for so long. If Lisha had been waiting for a way to reconnect with Aliza, *The Last Marilyn Monroe* would have become the key, quietly unlocking the door to her inner being. Through it, she felt her grandmother's presence once more.

Gazing at the image of Mailyn Monroe in the painting, Lisha felt the energy of Aliza's love transcending time and space, binding them together once again. The unspoken longing and regrets she carried finally found a place to rest. It was a sensation akin to Lisha gazed at Marilyn in the painting, and for a moment, she felt Aliza's love transcending time and space, drawing them together once more. The unspoken longing and regrets she had carried in her heart seemed to find solace and resolution. It was a feeling akin to "what you seek is seeking you." This profound realization resonated deeply within her soul through the interplay of abstract color cubes and the figurative image in the painting. Lisha felt that the painting's purpose was to awaken her—to make her understand the love, courage, and faith Aliza represented in her life and to reveal the ultimate calling of her destiny.

James Smith

The bustling evening streets of Dumbo were alive with energy, filled with stylish young people and vibrant graffiti murals radiating the neighborhood's unique artistic charm. Outside a restaurant, a street musician riffed on his guitar, the wistful melody mingling with the night and the glow of city lights, creating an ambiance of introspection.

James deeply resonated with Lisha's description of her grandmother Aliza's past life. He told her his grandfather was a successful businessman who traveled to Shanghai, China, in the 1940s to trade. At that time, Shanghai was the "Pearl of the Orient," a melting pot of Eastern and Western cultures and a paradise for adventurers. His grandfather lived in Shanghai for several years. He meticulously documented his fascination with the city in his diaries—from the bustling Bund to the serene cafés in the French Concession and the antique shops hidden in narrow alleyways. During his years in Shanghai, he amassed wealth through import-export trade. He acquired a collection of exquisite Chinese antiques, including delicate blue-and-white porcelain, intricately carved wooden screens, and works by renowned Chinese calligraphers. After the Communist Party took over China in 1949, all American businessmen were forced to leave, and James' grandfather had to bid farewell to the city he loved, never to return.

James grew up in the affluent Westchester suburbs of New York, enjoying a life of privilege. However, his interest lay not in the family business but in the Chinese antiques displayed in his grandfather's home. These objects filled him with curiosity, and he often pestered his grandfather to tell stories about Shanghai. The China described in his grandfather's diaries became a utopia in James' childhood imagination.

After his grandfather's passing, James became determined to visit China. During his sophomore year in college, he took a gap year to travel and explore the places his grandfather had mentioned. His journey eventually brought him to Shanghai. Standing on the Bund, gazing at the modern skyscrapers of Lujiazui across the Huangpu River, he felt a twinge of disappointment. The ultramodern metropolis bore little resemblance to the "Paris of the East" his grandfather had described. When he crossed to Lujiazui and looked back at the Bund, his disappointment deepened. The grand buildings that once defined the old Shanghai skyline now seemed dwarfed by the towering skyscrapers behind them, their former splendor reduced to a backdrop for modernity. The ambition and dreams his grandfather had once rooted in Shanghai seemed to have vanished along with the city's old charm.

Years passed, and James' connection to China faded into the recesses of his memory. Yet fate took a turn when he met Lisha. Her stories about her grandmother Aliza and her passion for art revived his long-dormant fascination with his grandfather's China. Through Lisha, he felt as though a door to the past had been reopened. Her love for art and Aliza's life story reawakened his childhood longing, bringing his grandfather's tales to life.

James told Lisha, "Even though we haven't known each other for long, I feel an unexplainable sense of belonging when I'm with you. It's as if our meeting was predestined. You've brought the Shanghai of my grandfather's stories back to life, and even the antiques that once felt cold and lifeless now seem to breathe with the warmth of his memories."

Hearing this, Lisha couldn't help but marvel at the concept of fate. She firmly believed in Bert Hellinger's family constellations theory, which posits that family inheritance and destiny span three generations. The fact that James' grandfather had lived in Shanghai during the same period as her grandmother Aliza felt like more than a coincidence. Though their ancestors' lives had never intersected, both pursued dreams in a city heralded as the "Paris of the East," leaving imprints of an era's transformation. For James and Lisha, Shanghai was more than a historical reference; it was a shared emotional anchor.

This conversation deepened their bond. Though intangible, the warmth of their connection was undeniable. Lisha, who had been sitting across from James, moved to sit beside him. James instinctively put his arm around her shoulders. Lisha took out her phone and showed James a few photos.

"These are a few sketches my grandmother Aliza drew," Lisha said. "She gave them to me as a keepsake when I left for the U.S. They're the only pieces of her artwork that remain."

The photos included a self-portrait of Aliza and two watercolor depictions of Shanghai street scenes, all brimming with the vintage charm of that era. James studied the paintings intently, wondering if this was how Shanghai had appeared to his grandfather all those years ago.

Reflecting on the art, Lisha said, "You know, '*The Last Marilyn Monroe*' reminds me of my grandmother Alisha. Especially the expression—it's so beautiful on the surface but carries an undercurrent of melancholy. Isn't it funny how life works? I never imagined I'd come across such a masterpiece at that gallery. Sometimes, when you see a painting or hear a song for the first time, it feels like something you've known forever, like love at first sight."

James chuckled, "I felt that way the first time I saw you. Like we've known each other forever."

Lisha playfully scolded, "I'm talking about art! True art has that kind of magnetic pull."

James sipped his wine, his gaze fixed on Lisha. At that moment, he couldn't describe the feeling surging through him. Their conversation had unveiled a connection he hadn't fully understood before, one that now felt undeniable. He was overwhelmed by an all-encompassing love for her. Unable to resist, he murmured, "But beauty can have that pull, too." At that moment, Lisha was everything to James.

Lisha, more serious now, replied, "Sometimes, it feels like a song or a painting can awaken a soul across lifetimes. I feel like that painting awakened something in me."

James suddenly said, "I get it now. That feeling I had when I saw you for the first time—that was my soul being awakened. You're the one who was meant to do that."

Lisha gave him a gentle push and laughed. "I'm being serious! I decided to buy that painting, no matter the cost, because I could feel its energy. This painting features a unique artistic language, painting each cube as if writing calligraphy to form a portrait of Marilyn Monroe. Up close, it's abstract, but from a distance, it's vividly realistic. The contrast is stunning. Of all the art I've seen, this piece is unforgettable, like it belongs among the great masters."

James mused, "That painting truly captures Mailyn Monroe's melancholy. She struggled with depression, which ran in her family—

her mother and relatives suffered from it, and in her later years, she seemed overwhelmed by it too."

Lisha agreed, "She never received the emotional validation she craved. From the start, she was packaged as a sex symbol—her beauty and sensuality drew endless admiration, but no one took the time to understand who she was. She was a creative, literary soul trapped in the image of a seductive icon, and the disparity between her outer and inner worlds ultimately destroyed her. My aunt Molly once wrote an article about Mailyn Monroe, saying, 'Mailyn Monroe, like any beautiful woman, had deep insecurities rooted in an unhappy childhood, a turbulent past, and her dependency on love and male approval. In Hollywood, a place teeming with starlets competing for attention, Mailyn Monroe was both angel and devil, a mature peach with an irresistible exterior but an insecure child within, always yearning for validation.'"

James was about to respond when Lisha, her mood suddenly somber, added, "Imagine a little girl whose mother is institutionalized, leaving her to be passed around between foster homes without stability or love. Once, when she called a foster mother 'Mom,' she was harshly reprimanded, 'You know better than anyone—I'm not your mother!'"

James's voice grew heavy. "That's heartbreaking, worse than that little robot in"A.I. Artificial Intelligence" going around asking, 'Are you my mother?' Later, when she married playwright Arthur Miller, she was attracted by his intellect. But even he exploited her celebrity status. And then there was President Kennedy—another man who used her. In the end, whether it was an overdose or foul play, I think she truly died of a broken heart."

Lisha looked at James in surprise, "I didn't expect you to know so much about Mailyn Monroe."

James smiled, "I love movies, and Mailyn Monroe is one of my favorite actresses. In college, I went through a phase where I watched all her films—and countless other American classics."

Lisha lit up, "My aunt and I both adore Mailyn Monroe. When I arrived in New York, she said the best way to understand America was through its movies. Living in her apartment, we watched old films daily, including all of Marilyn Mailyn Monroe's and probably over a hundred others. Our favorite was *Casablanca*."

James offered, "If you buy that painting, let me cover half the cost. Consider it my share in the investment."

Lisha teased, "Oh, you want a stake in my family? Too cheap an offer!"

James laughed, "You're too smart for me. I admit, I want to be your Mr. Mo."

Lisha smiled but said firmly, "But I'm not Aliza. My Mr. Mo must be braver, stronger, and more committed to love."

Suddenly, James knelt on one knee before her and said, "Lisha, from the moment I saw you, I knew I loved you. I can't imagine life without you. Will you marry me?"

Caught off guard, Lisha pulled him up, her expression serious, "James, this isn't something to joke about."

James looked hurt. "I'm not joking."

Lisha softened, "In Chinese, we say, 'Water must flow before the channel forms,' We'll wait until the water flows."

James seemed puzzled, trying to decipher her words.

Just then, a melancholic tune from the street musician caught Lisha's attention. She turned to James, "This melody reminds me of the songs my grandmother Alizaloved—so tender, with a tinge of sorrow, just like the rivers of Jiangnan."

James asked, "You always mention Jiangnan. What is it?"

Lisha laughed, teasing James, "The Jiangnan depicted in Tang and Song poetry is somewhat akin to Jianghu, the world of martial arts masters that we often talk about—it's just a sense, a certain feeling."

James felt a bit confused. Could it be that both Jiangnan and Jianghu are states of mind—an elusive presence that can be sensed but not fully explained in words?

Lisha changed the subject with a smile, "By the way, James, I've considered revisiting your museum after work. I need to see if my Mailyn Monroe painting truly holds its own against those in the collection."

James said, "Then let me invite you to a private tour after the museum closes. It's more meaningful—many stunning works can only be truly appreciated in silence."

Lisha's eyes sparkled, "That sounds amazing. An after-hour private tour at the museum must be magical."

24

Chapter II. **The Last Marilyn Monroe**

A Bond Between Father and Daughter

A large oil painting of Marilyn Monroe dominates one wall of Lisha's apartment. It is positioned beside the sofa and towers over the entire space.

The one-bedroom apartment offers a stunning view of midtown Manhattan's skyline. At six in the morning, the rising sun bathes the tops of skyscrapers in golden light, creating a picturesque scene framed by Lisha's floor-to-ceiling windows.

Sipping her coffee, Lisha glanced outside at the golden-hued cityscape while setting up a Zoom call with her parents back in China.

"Dad," Lisha said, "Did you see the photo I sent you last night? I bought an amazing painting. Look, you can see part of it behind me."

The living room of a northern Chinese city apartment had a window that revealed the faint silhouette of distant mountains. Lisha's father sat at the table, Zooming with his daughter, while her mother, Mo Hua, brought freshly prepared dishes to the table.

"Dad, Mom," Lisha said with a smile, "did you see the photo I sent last night? I bought an incredible painting—it's right behind me."

Her father flipped through his phone while her mother, Mo Hua, set the dinner table, responding casually, "Yes, we saw it! That painting is remarkable, better than anything your dad's art academy has ever exhibited."

Her father frowned slightly. "You called just to talk about a painting? You haven't Zoomed us in ages."

"I've been so busy lately," Lisha explained. "Ever since starting my company, every day has been about meeting clients. I didn't have to worry about client acquisition when I worked in an office. But now, every client needs me and my partner Martin to handle them personally."

Mo Hua added, "That Marilyn painting is gorgeous—better than any of your dad's art exhibitions."

Her father bristled. "What are you talking about? Are you saying our art academy can't compare to some unknown painter in New York?" He continued to scroll through his phone, stopping as he looked closer at the photo and video Lisha had sent.

"This painting is exceptional," he admitted. "You do have a good eye."

Lisha beamed, "Hearing that from you makes me feel much more confident. By the way, this artist also emigrated from China in the late '80s and has been in New York for decades. Just because you haven't heard of him doesn't mean he isn't renowned."

Her father retorted, "Are you implying I judge art solely by domestic standards?"

Lisha laughed, "Art is a product of the soul. It needs to move people and evoke beauty. Out here, no one cares what academy you graduated from or who your mentor was."

Sensing the tension, Mo Hua quickly interjected, "How's it going with James? Not to pressure you, but you're already thirty-six—before you know it, you'll be forty."

Lisha chuckled, "As you put it, I sound like an unwanted spinster."

Professor Li couldn't help but chuckle, "Don't listen to your mom's nonsense. Our daughter is talented, beautiful, a top graduate from a prestigious art program back home, with an MBA from Columbia Business School. Now, she's making her mark on Wall Street in New York. What's there to worry about?"

Lisha laughed at how her father had summed up her entire life in just a few sentences. "Haha, Dad, you get me." Turning to her mother, she added, "James is great, but he's too by the book. He lacks the adventurous spirit I admire."

Mo Hua sighed, "Your dad was adventurous, too. Left a secure position as a state art academy professor to run a private museum and mingle with young contemporary artists. What could I do?"

Her father ignored the jab; his eyes fixed on the painting behind Lisha in the Zoom call.

"Here," Lisha said, picking up her iPad to give them a closer look. She adjusted the camera towards the Marilyn Monroe painting and explained, "Look at the intricate details. You see these colorful abstract cubes up close, but it becomes a lifelike portrait when you step back."

Her father leaned in, his expression tinged with surprise, "Impressive. This technique is unique. The color is precise, and the artist must have a solid foundation to pull this off."

Lisha felt a surge of pride. Her father, known for his discerning taste, rarely praised contemporary art. Yet here he was, impressed by her choice—a validation she hadn't anticipated but deeply appreciated.

"Dad," Lisha ventured, "don't you think there's something in Marilyn's expression that resembles Grandma Aliza ?"

Mo Hua set down her utensils and peered at the screen. After a moment, she exclaimed, "There's a resemblance! Especially in the eyes—there's a subtle sadness there."

Her father's expression softened as he mused, "It's rare to capture such emotion in a painting. A true work of art connects with the viewer emotionally—that's priceless."

Lisha grinned, "Mom, I remember a photo of Grandma taken at Sam Sanzetti's studio in Shanghai. Do you still have it?"

Mo Hua shook her head, "Molly took it to New York years ago."

Three Women, Countless Stories

On a calm and breezy day, Lisha arranged to meet her aunt Molly at a restaurant near her place. Usually, they would meet at Lisha's apartment, but this time, Molly mentioned she would bring a friend along, so Lisha chose a favorite restaurant nearby.

When Molly arrived in New York, Lisha was still in kindergarten. After earning her master's degree in television production at Brooklyn College, Molly worked for an American television company and was later sent back to China to expand the company's market. Lisha vividly remembered her aunt telling her fascinating stories about New York, taking her to upscale clubs and five-star hotels frequented by foreigners, and even letting her visit her office. Growing up with her aunt, Lisha spoke English fluently, without any trace of an accent, often chatting effortlessly with foreign guests. Later, Molly married and returned to New York, occasionally visiting China.

After Lisha was admitted to an art academy, she expressed her desire to study abroad. Molly advised her to complete her degree before considering moving to New York. In 2010, Lisha enrolled in Columbia Business School for an MBA and moved into Molly's suburban home. After Molly divorced, she relocated to Manhattan. By then, Lisha had graduated and found a job at a major Wall Street firm, allowing her to rent her place.

Molly worked as a marketing manager for an independent publisher in Manhattan and was also writing a nonfiction memoir about their family history. She brought all the family's old photographs to New York to aid her research.

Lisha sat by the restaurant's window, sunlight streaming through the glass panes and casting colorful shadows on the tables and floor. Bathed in light and shadow, Lisha looked as radiant as a painting.

Molly entered the restaurant with a stylishly dressed, elegant woman in her early forties, following a handsome young host. The moment Molly spotted Lisha, her face lit up with an exuberant smile. Despite being in her fifties, Molly maintained a figure as slim and graceful as in her youth, and her appearance seemed even more striking than when she was younger.

Lisha watched her aunt Molly walk toward her across the restaurant, and for a moment, she seemed to catch a glimpse of a young Aliza. Molly bore a striking resemblance to Aliza, her features reflecting their quarter-Western heritage. Though middle-aged, Molly's youthful energy still made her stand out in the crowd like a crane among chickens. In contrast, Lisha's mother took after her father, Mr. Mo, with distinctly Chinese features.

"Darling!" Molly called out to Lisha from a distance. Her enthusiastic greeting completely ignored the tranquil elegance of the restaurant and its softly chatting patrons. Waving energetically, she radiated vitality and drew diners' attention as if a celebrity had entered the room.

"My aunt is such a drama queen," Lisha thought wryly. Molly had a flair for theatrics, both in public and private, as if her life were a grand performance. She seemed the perfect person to write Aliza's story, and her passionate personality and familial connection promise a vivid narrative.

As soon as she sat down, Molly introduced the elegant woman beside her, "This is Julia, the renowned art columnist for The Times. She specializes in art commentary, news, and stories."

After exchanging greetings with Julia, Lisha quickly asked her aunt, "Did you bring Grandma's photos?"

"Of course," Molly said, pulling a black photo album from her bag. The album, though still elegant with faint embossed patterns on its cover, showed signs of age with worn edges. "Here's a collection of Grandma's old family photos."

The album, from 1930s Shanghai, featured a protective layer of translucent paper over each photograph. As Lisha carefully flipped through its pages, childhood memories surfaced. She remembered her grandmother showing her this album like a storybook, filled with family portraits and snapshots of Aliza's life. Through these photos, Lisha had come to know Aliza's story. Each time her grandmother recounted tales of 1940s Shanghai, Lisha would find echoes of those times within the photos.

Lisha's gaze eventually settled on a portrait of Aliza, taken at the renowned Sam Sanzetti Photo Studio. She studied it closely.

Molly remarked, "The artist who created *The Last Marilyn Monroe* has such a remarkable style. If we commissioned him to paint a portrait of Aliza, I bet he could bring her beauty back to life— in full color."

"That's a fantastic idea," Lisha agreed, "Ordinary oil paintings lack uniqueness, but his technique, combining Eastern calligraphic strokes with Western color aesthetics, makes his work truly collectible."

Molly said, "It's such a pity you didn't pursue an art career. With your understanding of art and natural intuition, you could've been very successful—and you could have supported underappreciated artists like him."

Lisha replied, "Actually, I've thought about starting an art fund. Maybe that's my dream."

Molly beamed, "If you start one, I'll be your first investor!"

Touched, Lisha said, "Auntie, you've always been my biggest supporter."

Julia glanced through Aliza's old photo album. She exclaimed, "She looks somewhat similar to a young Marilyn Monroe—radiantly charming on the surface, yet exuding a profound innocence at her core."

Lisha agreed, saying, "The most important thing is that while it's easy to paint a beautiful woman, capturing her expression is far more challenging—especially using this form of calligraphic brushstrokes. That's exactly why *The Last Marilyn Monroe* moved me so deeply."

Molly enthusiastically added, "Lisha majored in art in college and earned an MBA from Columbia before moving into finance. Truly talented."

Julia smiled, "Switching from art to finance is a bold move. I majored in literature and earned a master's in art history, so my career as an art columnist feels more aligned with my studies."

Lisha sighed, "My father was a university art professor before resigning to become the director of a private art museum, which gave my mom constant headaches. After graduating from art school, I decided to study business in New York. I didn't want to pursue art any further because, back in China, the art world was too tied to academies and mentors. It was nearly impossible to succeed if you didn't attend a prestigious academy or study under a famous professor. It's not an environment conducive to artistic creativity."

Julia nodded, "It's similar here, even if the rules are different. An artist's success often depends on gallery representation. A good gallery can elevate an artist to fame, but a mediocre one adds a name to its roster. That's why galleries often choose young artists—they have the potential to grow in value over time, benefiting the gallery."

Lisha pulled out her phone and showed Julia a photo of *The Last Marilyn Monroe*. "I recently bought this oil painting. It's exceptional. Take a look."

Julia examined the photo intently. "It's truly remarkable and beautiful," she said.

Lisha smiled, "You must come to my place and see the original. Photos and videos don't do it justice."

When Julia learned that the artist was neither represented by a gallery nor recognized in the art world but lived reclusively, painting what he loved, she sighed, "That must be incredibly difficult," she said, "For an artist to stay true to their path without being influenced by galleries or seeking fame requires immense perseverance and courage."

Lisha asked tentatively, "Could you write an article introducing this artist and his work? I think he needs support."

Julia gently shook her head and said, "Even though I'm the lead writer for the arts column, most of what I write and the people I interview are the usual names everyone in the art world knows. Otherwise, the newspaper bosses won't be happy if my articles don't get enough readers. Over time, even my position as lead writer could be at risk!"

Lisha fell silent, "I see. No wonder people say the art world is like a sealed iron barrel—once you're in when you're young, you'd better not step out. Otherwise, it's a dead end."

The waiter began serving their main courses, placing each dish on the table as the conversation continued.

Lisha remarked, "I just can't understand how taping a banana to a wall can sell for over $6 million, yet such a stunning oil painting only sells for a few tens of thousands—and people still think it's overpriced. Is the world truly this upside down?"

Julia replied, "First, modern art isn't about craftsmanship anymore—it's about concepts. Second, art is all about trends. That banana sold because it was a sensation, not because of its artistic value. If your painting could be marketed as a trending piece, it could easily sell for millions."

Molly said, "That's why everyone wants to be a social media influencer. These days, the value of art isn't about quality but buzz."

"I have an idea," Lisha said. "What if we secretly put this painting in

James's museum and see how the public reacts?"

Molly laughed, "Exactly! If a banana can go viral, why not this?"

Julia chuckled, "You're talking about challenging the establishment!"

Lisha smirked, "What establishment? It's all just a money game. Some make the rules, and others play. Why can't we be the rule-makers?"

Julia nodded, "That reminds me of Banksy. In 2004, he snuck one of his works into the Louvre and hung it on the wall. For eight days, visitors admired it like a masterpiece until staff finally discovered it and removed it."

Molly laughed heartily, "Yes, he pulled a similar stunt at the MET. In 2013, he had someone sell his authentic works in Central Park for $60 apiece. Only a handful of people bought them, thinking they were fakes. The next day, Banksy revealed the truth on his website, and those $60 pieces were resold for $250,000 each."

Lisha said, "Exactly, art needs to break boundaries, just like the Australian artist Ben Butcher, who snuck into Melbourne's National Gallery of Victoria and hung his work on the wall. The label on his piece read: 'We live in an age where monolithic cultural institutions no longer have a monopoly over the distribution of ideas. Media that was once only accessible to a privileged few is now freely available to the masses, and direct action and self-publishing are now unprecedentedly possible.'"

The three women laughed and grew increasingly animated, chatting enthusiastically and passionately about their views on art. Amid the lively discussion, an idea began to take shape in Lisha's mind—a plan to secretly place an artwork in a museum.

The Old Master

Seated on the subway heading from Manhattan to Brooklyn, Lisha and Molly discussed the artist behind *The Last Marilyn Monroe*. Molly, glowing with excitement, shared how she had leveraged every connection she could think of in the art world, even enlisting her fiancé, private investigator WilliamGold, to uncover the painter's story. According to her, the artist's technique was extraordinary, his talent unparalleled, and his unique, challenging style unmatched. Despite rarely making public appearances, the art world was never short on stories about him, and he was respectfully referred to as "the old master ."

Molly animatedly recounted his past. "Did you know he came to New York in the 1980s and was a big name in the art scene? But then he vanished. When he reappeared, his style had transformed into this unique calligraphic cube painting."

"Why did he disappear?" Lisha asked curiously.

"Some say he didn't like the pretentious games of the art world," Molly said mysteriously. "Others claim he went into business to make money. But who knows the truth?"

"Wow!" Lisha exclaimed with a laugh, "You are playing detective this time."

Molly raised her eyebrows proudly. "With William 's help digging into records and through my sources, I pieced together his legendary life."

The old master was born in Nanjing. His parents were sent to the "May Seventh Cadre School" for labor during his childhood. His parents had no choice but to send him to his grandmother's home in rural Wuxi. In a world without toys, surrounded only by endless farmland and rustic simplicity, he often lay alone on the grass, gazing at the sky, watching the clouds shift and imagining them transforming into dragons, fish, or rabbits.

Over time, he surrendered his soul to the quiet power and natural beauty found in the solitude of Wuxi's countryside. This harmony between silence and nature became the latent source of his artistic energy. When the time came for that energy to erupt, it became the driving force behind his art.

Those solitary years in the farmland of Wuxi nurtured his keen eye for detail and boundless imagination and shaped his independent, introspective nature.

His grandmother, a devout Buddhist, often told him, "Amitabha, good and evil will always find their reward." She shared stories of karma, instilling in him a belief that every step in life planted seeds for the future. This philosophy profoundly influenced his art, imbuing his works with the depth of Eastern thought.

As a young boy, he displayed extraordinary artistic talent, earning the affection of his neighbors and teachers. One neighbor, a retired art professor who played the erhu, taught him to paint and introduced him to music. This blend of music and painting became vital to his creative foundation. He once said, "Music and painting are inseparable in my life. Perhaps this is fate."

During his formative years, China was opening up to the world, exposing young minds to Western literature and art. For him, modern poetry offered a contrast to the beauty of Tang and Song poetry, inspiring a fresh perspective on the world. As a teenager, he and his friends would gather in a café, emulating bourgeois intellectuals and discussing everything from the Seven Sages of the Bamboo Grove to James Joyce, T.S. Eliot, Su Dongpo, and Sisyphus. "One friend once said we should place our eyes in the air and look down on ourselves. As a young painter with a vivid imagination, you can guess how that idea struck me."

Around this time, an art book from his professor opened his eyes to the vastness of contemporary art, especially the styles emerging from New York. Abandoning his acceptance to Nanjing Academy of Arts, he left for New York, his heart torn between apprehension and hope.

Arriving in New York, he experienced a cultural and artistic shock. Immersed in the avant-garde scenes of Greenwich Village and the Lower East Side, he felt lost and exhilarated. To make ends meet, he worked for a construction company while painting in his spare time. Limited resources pushed him to innovate, and he incorporated materials from construction sites into his works, blending abstract styles with elements of Eastern philosophy.

His art soon caught the attention of a German gallery, which exhibited his works across Europe. In 1990, a German museum

I see Brooklyn, I think of her and regret that she never reunited with her family here."

Lisha was also moved by Molly's sentiment and said, "This reminds me of the film *Brooklyn*, which portrays Irish immigrants' emotional struggles between their homeland and New York. No one has written about the stories of us immigrants from mainland China who left everything behind. If Aliza and Mr. Mo had come to Brooklyn back then, their story might have been rewritten. At the very least, Mr. Mo might still be alive."

Tears glistened in Molly's eyes as she replied in a low voice, "When my father passed away, I was only two years old—I have no memory of him at all. My whole life has been one without a father, and the pain that comes with it is hard to put into words. Aliza raised your mother and me through such difficult times; it wasn't easy. That's why I've spent my whole life wanting to understand my parents' experiences and emotional journeys, to give myself some closure and comfort."

Lisha gently embraced her aunt and said softly, "I understand. Bert Hellinger talks about intergenerational trauma and how family pain can carry on for three generations, shaping us emotionally, psychologically, and even physically throughout our lives. We must consciously work to change these three aspects to break free from the cycle of family pain. How is your family book coming along? I'm looking forward to reading it soon."

Molly smiled mysteriously, "It's nearly done. Over the years, I've gathered so much history, including fragments of Aliza's diary."

"Really?" Lisha exclaimed, wide-eyed.

"Yes," Molly replied, "I found folded papers hidden in her photo album. When I opened them, they were in her handwriting—snippets about her life in Shanghai. They read like diary entries."

Lisha eagerly said, "Let me see them!"

Molly teased, "You'll have to read my book—it's all in there. Did you know Alizasecretly had a crush on a boy from her French school who loved painting? He never knew."

Lisha laughed, "No wonder she painted watercolors. I especially love her vibrant sketches of old Shanghai streets."

As the two talked, the subway reached their intended stop, and Molly urged Lisha to get off quickly. They exited the station and strolled down a chaotic yet artistically energetic street filled with graffiti.

Lisha returned to the gallery where she had purchased the painting, hoping to establish direct contact with the old master and uncover more of his story.

The gallery's director, a graceful Chinese woman named Tao Hua, a notable curator, greeted Lisha warmly. "I'd love to help you," Tao Hua said kindly, "but the old master has been reclusive for many years and avoids outside disturbances. However, if you have specific inquiries, we can try to reach out on your behalf."

Tao Hua explained that the old master entrusted his works to their gallery because he trusted their nonprofit mission. He believed that the gallery approached his work purely from an artistic perspective and was committed to promoting authentic artistic values. This made him feel that his work was genuinely being seen.

"Being seen!" Lisha repeated the phrase. She suddenly realized that this "being seen" meant the recognition of the uniqueness of an artist's language and the essence of their art. This kind of acknowledgment is the understanding every artist longs for throughout life.

"Do you know why he painted this particular portrait of Marilyn Monroe?" Lisha asked.

"He has painted many portraits of Marilyn Monroe, most of which have been collected. This one, however, is the largest and most recent. It hasn't been purchased yet because the old master believes the collector destined for this piece must truly understand it. He once said, 'The collector already exists; I don't know who they are yet. But when they appear, our souls will connect, and they will understand the painting's meaning.'"

Tao Hua smiled at Lisha, "Since you've acquired this piece, Lisha, I'd love to hear your interpretation of its significance."

Lisha paused before responding, her tone contemplative, "At first, I was struck by its uniqueness. The style was unlike anything I'd ever seen—breathtakingly beautiful and deeply moving. This painting reminded me of my grandmother, Aliza. She was as stunning as Mailyn Monroe but had endured countless hardships. After losing her beloved husband, she came to realize that life exists in two forms: the physical body and the soul. When the body perishes, the soul remains. She often told me, 'Even if I'm no longer here, my soul will always be with you.' The moment I saw this painting, I felt a profound connection—a sense that my grandmother's soul had touched mine."

Lisha hesitated, wondering if she was revealing too much to a stranger. Fully engrossed in the story, Tao Hua gently prompted, "And then?"

Lisha smiled faintly, "I want to understand the artist's thoughts behind creating this work. Often, our actions are guided by the soul. Our physical senses are limited and unable to perceive what lies beyond the three-dimensional. Perhaps our conversation today was fated—this meeting could be a reunion from another lifetime."

Molly chimed in, "I've been writing a book about Aliza's spiritual side. She once told me about her first meeting with my father. She described it as a moment of profound connection, transcending time itself. She said, 'Sometimes, a seemingly random encounter feels inexplicably deep as if we've known each other forever. Without introductions or explanations, we understand each other's pasts and hearts. Perhaps it's a kind of unspoken destiny, a story whose ending we already know before it begins. And we are the protagonists of that story. Our recognition and familiarity with each other transcend time as if we've journeyed through lifetimes to reunite.'"

Lisha exclaimed, "Exactly! It's that kind of feeling—no words are needed. Even a shared glance feels like unlocking a hidden memory. Our connection feels preordained from a past life, and meeting in this one is merely the continuation of an unfinished bond."

Tao Hua, moved by their reflections, remarked, "Aliza must have been extraordinary, just like both of you. I'm so glad to have met you."

Molly laughed, "I'm just writing my mother's biography—not extraordinary. But my niece, Lisha, is something else! Always talking like a mystic!"

Tao Hua chuckled and pulled out her phone, adding Lisha and Molly on WeChat. She invited them to return anytime for discussions about art. "Our gallery often hosts art symposiums," she said. "I hope you'll both join us."

Before Lisha left, Tao Hua gifted her the only published catalog of the old master's work. It included an introduction to the artist and images of his early and recent paintings. Through this catalog, Lisha realized that the old master's choice to remain reclusive stemmed from his pursuit of pure art.

In his youth, the old master participated in numerous mainstream art exhibitions but gradually became disillusioned with the commercialized art world. He felt that market dynamics stripped art of its authenticity. He rejected many lucrative offers and remained steadfast in following his creative vision.

The old master worked in isolation, retreating into a meditative state to immerse himself fully in his art. He described this process as entering a harmonious inner world, where the vastness of the universe met the minutiae of existence.

One quote in the catalog caught Lisha's attention: "When you are moved by my work, it is your soul responding to my perseverance." As she closed the catalog, Lisha felt an overwhelming sense of kinship, as though she had found a kindred spirit.

As they were leaving the gallery, Lisha noticed the background music playing inside. She paused and asked Tao Hua, "Is this a guitar melody?"

Tao Hua smiled, "Yes, it's by a musician whose work I love. I often play it here."

Lisha's eyes lit up, "I thought so! This musician sometimes performs outside the MET. That's why the tune sounded so familiar."

Outside the gallery, Molly teased, "You've got sharp ears, recognizing the musician from just a melody!"

Lisha grinned, "True art speaks to the soul, whether music or painting. This melody is so distinctly Jiangnan—it's enchanting. Let's head to the riverside park and catch the sunset."

As twilight fell over Brooklyn, Lisha and Molly gazed at the Brooklyn Bridge, which stretched across the water toward Manhattan's skyline. The fiery hues of the sunset painted the sky and reflected on the rippling water, creating a mesmerizing scene.

Chapter III. **The Night at MET**

After closing hours, the Metropolitan Museum of Art stood in profound silence. Along the dimly lit gallery walls, timeless masterpieces seemed to shimmer with ethereal energy, as though the spirit of each artist had traveled across centuries—sometimes millennia—to reach the present. The atmosphere was almost palpable, a testament to the enduring power of their genius.

Lisha and James walked alongside Jonathan, who worked in the museum's Modern and Contemporary Art Department. As they moved through the quiet halls, their conversation flowed naturally. Jonathan, a tall, slender man in his late thirties, wore gold-rimmed glasses that added to his scholarly demeanor. He and James had known each other since college, and it was James who had initially recommended Jonathan for his role at the MET.

Over the years, the two had often shared drinks and long discussions about art, philosophy, and life. In truth, much of James's understanding of art came from Jonathan's in-depth explanations and anecdotes. Profoundly passionate and extraordinarily knowledgeable about art, Jonathan often felt like an unrecognized talent. His innovative perspectives and philosophies about art left him at odds with the mainstream yet undeniably set him apart.

To Lisha, someone like Jonathan, working in the contemporary art department of such a prestigious institution, was nothing short of extraordinary. She couldn't help but wonder what Jonathan might think of the Marilyn Monroe painting she had recently purchased. Yet, she hesitated to bring it up, unsure how to steer the conversation in that direction. Instead, she attentively listened as Jonathan elaborated on the exhibits they had just viewed.

Finally, they stopped before one of Andy Warhol's silkscreen prints. Lisha paused, examining the artwork intently.

"My favorites are his Marilyn Monroe and Chairman Mao pieces," Lisha said, unable to hold back. "For those of us from China, these works hold special significance."

Jonathan looked at Lisha with interest. He had always thought that a driven woman like Lisha, with her background of studying and working in New York, seemed like a mismatch for someone as conventional as James. Now, he was curious to hear her thoughts.

Lisha explained, "My grandmother lived during Marilyn Monroe's time. As two bustling port cities, Shanghai and New York were similar back then. For my parents' generation, born in the 1950s and

'60s, Chairman Mao was an omnipresent backdrop, symbolizing the revolutionary era. By the time my generation was born in the '80s and '90s, we had seen Marilyn Monroe's movies and the 'decadent capitalism' she represented gradually becoming a reality in Chinese society. In a way, Marilyn Monroe and Chairman Mao are emblems of two vastly different eras."

"Interesting!" Jonathan remarked. "Andy Warhol created his Marilyn diptych in 1962. His silkscreen prints began that August, coinciding with Marilyn Monroe's death. Her star power inspired him to create his first Marilyn silkscreen."

"What a coincidence!" Lisha said with a laugh. "I just bought an oil painting of Marilyn Monroe. What do you think of it?" She pulled out her phone and showed Jonathan the piece, zooming in and out to highlight the changes in detail.

"Look," Lisha said, "the technique is fascinating. Up close, it's abstract, but from a distance, it's completely realistic."

Jonathan studied the artwork closely, nodding and repeatedly saying, "Interesting!" Finally, he asked, "Do I know this artist?"

Lisha shook her head, "Probably not. He's not on your radar yet because he rarely appears in public. He lives in seclusion in the countryside, almost like a hermit." She knew someone like Jonathan, immersed in MET's elite art circles, would primarily be familiar with globally recognized artists.

"Oh," Jonathan replied, "But his work is on par with the artists I do know. "It seems the city still harbors extraordinary talents I have yet to discover." Half joking and half serious, he was trying to save face. Indeed, after years in the museum, Jonathan felt like he lived in an ivory tower, disconnected from the vibrant art scenes beyond its walls.

Lisha said, "Why don't you and James come to my place someday to see the painting? Photos and videos just don't do it justice."

Jonathan agreed, "Absolutely. The presence of the original work is something no reproduction can capture. Artists imbue their work with an energy that only the original can convey."

"'Ying xiong suo jian lve tong!'" Lisha exclaimed in Chinese, her tone playful. Jonathan and James exchanged puzzled looks.

"It means 'Great minds think alike,'" Lisha laughed, noticing their confusion.

A while later, Jonathan excused himself, saying his wife was waiting for him at home for dinner. Lisha and James continued wandering through the empty museum.

Suddenly, Lisha leaned close to James and whispered, "What if I secretly placed a painting here right now? No one would notice. Tomorrow, everyone would think the museum had a new exhibit."

James chuckled, "If it's a small painting, maybe. But if it's something as large as *The Last Marilyn Monroe*, we'd have a problem—it's too heavy to move!"

Lisha replied, "A large painting has more presence. It can only truly shine in a museum."

At that moment, Lisha stopped mid-sentence, recalling her

conversation with Molly and Julia. A thought struck her: if she believed so strongly in *The Last Marilyn Monroe*, why not find a way to place it in MET? She was convinced that others would love the painting as much as she did. She wanted to test her theory.

But how could she possibly smuggle such a large piece into MET?

Noticing Lisha's sudden silence, James asked, "What are you thinking about?"

Lisha replied, "I'm thinking about how to sneak *The Last Marilyn Monroe* into the museum!"

James was taken aback. He had assumed Lisha was joking earlier, but now it seemed she was serious. He grew nervous. "A small painting might be easy, but a large one? That's difficult! Besides, why would you do it? It's not even your artwork. What's the point of taking such a big risk?"

Lisha looked at James in surprise. "The point is to prove that it's a great piece of art, deserving of a museum. I also want to see how many people, like me reject today's trend of 'conceptual gimmicks' in favor of appreciating stunning art. Haven't you ever wanted to do something bold, even risky, just once in your life?"

James fell silent, reflecting on her words. Suddenly, he understood why he found Lisha so captivating—she had a daring spirit that he lacked. In her twenties, Lisha had left her home country to start anew in New York. By contrast, he had never even traveled to Asia, let alone uprooted himself to begin life in a foreign land.

"You're right," James admitted. "I've always admired your courage

51

to embrace change while I've settled into a predictable life where 'no bad news is good news.'"

Lisha smiled, "I think I inherited my grandmother Aliza's fearless spirit—her refusal to compromise with life. Maybe this kind of determination runs in the family."

Lisha shared with James how Aliza loved painting and created watercolor depictions of Shanghai's old neighborhoods, scenes that no longer existed and were now historically valuable. Lisha had once tried to donate a few of Aliza's watercolors to a museum, only to be politely declined.

Lisha said, "Because she wasn't a famous artist, museums only collect and display big-name works. But one day, I want to challenge these so-called art rules. I don't care about an artist's fame or status—only about the quality of the work."

James put his arm around Lisha's shoulders. "Looks like I'll need to borrow some of your confidence and energy to find my courage."

Lisha smiled. She felt their energies had finally aligned, just as she had always felt a connection with Aliza's spirit. Their shared understanding gave her clarity about the past and confidence for the future. She gently rested her head on James's shoulder as they entered another hall. In the dim light of the museum, their silhouettes merged into one, fading into the distance.

Chapter IV. **The Party**

Lisha, wearing a flowing white chiffon dress, looked graceful and slim. Holding a glass of wine, she moved effortlessly among her guests. Since moving to this new apartment from Brooklyn, she had taken a liking to hosting small gatherings where she could chat with friends about art, literature, and life. Despite living in New York for years since leaving China, Lisha maintained close ties with her circle of friends, and her parties often felt like intellectual salons.

This evening's gathering, themed *The Last Marilyn Monroe*, was organized to showcase and discuss Lisha's recently purchased oil painting. Lisha loved the artwork and its evocative name, which seemed to resonate with something deep within her.

She would have loved to invite the artist behind the painting to attend the event and share the inspiration and philosophy behind the work. However, when she contacted the reclusive artist through her well-connected aunt, Molly, the old master politely declined. He lived on a farm in upstate New York and rarely participated in public art events.

Rather than feeling disappointed, Lisha found herself admiring the artist even more. To her, a creator who willingly distanced themselves from the hustle and bustle of society was the epitome of a revered recluse. In Chinese traditional culture, the concept of reclusion holds a deep-rooted history. Beyond monks and Taoists retreating to remote sanctuaries for meditation, Chinese scholars and painters have often captured the fleeting beauty of nature in landscape paintings, presenting a poetic vision of retreat. This sense of reclusion—leaving the worldly chaos behind to dwell in harmony with the broader serenity of nature—has inspired generations of artists, many of whom, upon reaching a certain age, choose to live in the countryside rather than urban centers to draw energy from the natural world.

Lisha was fond of an exhibition she once saw at the MET, which explored the theme of reclusion in art and literature. Reclusion, as she understood it, wasn't about rejecting the world but about forging deeper connections through art and poetry, fostering like-minded exchanges. She particularly loved the Preface to the Orchid Pavilion Gathering by Wang Xizhi, written during his retreat at the Orchid Pavilion. During that time, Wang Xizhi hosted a gathering of like-minded literati, all living reclusive lives, to drink wine and compose poetry. Amid the autumnal beauty, they reflected on the passage of time and the nature of life and death. Wang Xizhi immortalized the gathering with his calligraphy, which later became widely disseminated through reproductions.

The Orchid Pavilion gathering also became an enduring theme in Chinese painting. A notable example is Qian Gu's 1560 handscroll, which vividly depicts the convivial scenes of Wang Xizhi's gathering at the Orchid Pavilion, blending the poetic with the pictorial to eternalize the essence of reclusive living.

For *The Last Marilyn Monroe* gathering, Lisha had only invited a small group of close friends, including James, Jonathan, and his wife, Julia.

Jonathan introduced Julia to Lisha, "Julia is an art columnist who covers the latest happenings in the art world."

Lisha laughed warmly, "Oh, we've already met!" Jonathan was surprised, realizing he hadn't connected the dots. Julia had mentioned that she knew Lisha before, but he hadn't paid much attention, thinking she was referring to one of the many "Lisas" they knew.

Julia hugged Lisha and laughed, "There's nothing new in my column. Art reporting has become repetitive—just the same galleries, museums, and artists over and over again."

"That's what we Chinese call "Chao Lengfan" - reheating cold rice!" Molly exclaimed as she came running out of the kitchen to hug Julia and Jonathan. Molly had arrived with her fiancé, William Gold. The couple had recently gotten engaged, and Lisha had attended their engagement ceremony with James, where the two men had already met.

James handed Gold a glass of wine and introduced him to Jonathan. The three men started a conversation quickly, laughing and chatting as they sipped their drinks.

As more guests arrived, they gathered in the open kitchen and living room. A white sheet covered the painting on the wall, adding a sense of mystery to the evening.

Lisha tapped her wine glass to get everyone's attention. "Now, it's time for tonight's highlight: the unveiling of *The Last Marilyn Monroe*!" She shared how she first encountered the painting, her grandmother Aliza's tale, her parents' thoughts on the work, and her reflections.

The guests were captivated. Connecting a single painting to a family's history felt like serendipity—a word Lisha loved, representing the harmony of fate and timing. Anticipation grew as Lisha led everyone to the living room, instructing James and Jonathan to pull down the white sheet with the flair of a ribbon-cutting ceremony.

As the sheet fell, Marilyn Monroe's portrait emerged, taking everyone's breath away. The massive painting left the guests in awe as they gathered to examine it more closely. Jonathan moved back and forth, alternating between studying it up close and viewing it from afar.

Lisha said, "My living room is too small for this painting. The farther back you stand, the clearer it becomes. Try using your phones—it's even more striking on screen."

Taking her advice, the guests held up their phones, marveling at how Marilyn's image became even more vivid on the screens.

"Wow!" Julia exclaimed. "This is a masterpiece! I'd love to meet the artist."

Lisha laughed, "I only glimpsed a photo of him at the gallery's opening. He's the kind of artist who doesn't even attend his own openings. According to Molly, he's been a reclusive painter for over thirty years since coming to New York, and very few people know his story."

Julia said, "I know quite a few contemporary Chinese artists, but I've never heard of a reclusive one."

Holding a glass of wine, Molly squinted at the painting and said, "In Chinese culture, recluses are often the true masters, those who've transcended worldly distractions. This artist isn't ordinary. A friend of mine saw his work in the '90s when he was still young. His earlier pieces were influenced by various contemporary art movements but lacked a unique voice. After a decade-long hiatus, he reemerged with this distinct style. What you see now is the result of his quest for a personal artistic language."

Julia sighed, "The energy of this piece is immense. It expands your living room visually and emotionally."

Lisha said solemnly, "Edgar Degas once said, 'Art is not what you see but what you make others see.' This painting shows more than just Marilyn—it reveals her inner struggles and desires. Everyone who looks at it feels its impact. It would create an even greater ripple effect if displayed in a museum."

She turned to Jonathan and said, "This piece could hold its own in your museum. Imagine if all his works were displayed together in one gallery—it would be spectacular."

Jonathan nodded, "Degas's words are profound. If art isn't placed before the public, it becomes nothing."

With a wry smile, Julia added, "Then we must make it seen."

James was teasing Molly, saying, "Since this painter is a Chinese artist, you must be able to find him. You have such a vast network—who don't you know?"

Molly burst into laughter, nearly doubling over. "The people I know are mostly materialistic mortals, not necessarily spiritual masters."

At that moment, James noticed Lisha's gaze and quickly shifted his attention to her. "Why don't we start a crowdfunding campaign," he suggested, "so people can collectively buy this artist's works and then organize an exhibition to showcase them together?"

Lisha's business partner, Martin, commented, "This painting is impressive, but its commercial value matters just as much. If we orchestrate a large-scale publicity campaign, its market value could multiply several times. We could establish a fund, acquire the old master's works, and promote them heavily through various media channels. Once the market begins to clamor for the scarcity of his pieces, their value would skyrocket, and we could sell them off gradually. That would make us all very wealthy. However, this strategy would take years to execute and isn't guaranteed success. It would require the artist's full cooperation and a market willing to buy into the hype."

In his early fifities, a Dutch-American Wall Street investor, was

Lisha's business partner at her investment firm. Renowned for his shrewdness and exceptional judgment of people and projects, Martin often made successful investments. Since partnering with him, Lisha's ventures have consistently turned a profit.

Martin was also a master at saving money. He told Lisha, "Investing isn't about spending—it's about doing big things with little money. If you think of me every time you're about to spend, you'll never lose your money."

When Lisha purchased *The Last Marilyn Monroe*, Martin's advice came to mind. She knew he would never put his money into art. For Martin, art was something he could appreciate but never fully understand. He often joked that he had no artistic sense whatsoever. Whenever he attended an exhibition filled with bizarre and fantastical works, he would be completely at a loss as to what the artists were trying to convey. Once, a friend dragged him to an art show, teasing him, "You don't need to understand a thing. Just rest your chin on your hand, look thoughtful, and if anyone asks, say you've felt the artist's pain."

At that moment, Martin, looking at the painting Lisha had purchased, surprisingly understood its appeal. He remarked, "I don't sense the artist's pain; instead, it gives me peace and serenity." This rare moment of clarity sparked an idea for potential investment: acquiring the artwork at a low price, finding ways to increase its value through calculated hype, and eventually selling it at a much higher price. If, as Degas famously said, "Art is not what you see, but what you make others see," then Martin saw the capital acquisition and the potential for appreciation in value.

Julia whispered to Jonathan, "See, the difference in thinking between capitalists and artists is like night and day!"

Molly turned to Martin with a grin. "You know finance. If Lisha starts a fund with you, count me in. I see both the art and the money!"

The group burst into a lively discussion about the foundation. Some agreed with James' crowdfunding idea, and everyone enthusiastically shared their opinions.

Lisha turned to Jonathan and asked, "In your opinion, how does this painting compare to the works in the MET?"

Jonathan replied, "If we're talking about quality and craftsmanship, this painting is MET-worthy."

"I mean in terms of the essence, the intrinsic content of the work," Lisha clarified.

Jonathan nodded, "The painting itself is flawless. It has a unique artistic language."

Julia asked Jonathan, "Do you think this piece resembles Chuck Close's work?"

Jonathan shook his head decisively, his tone firm. "When I first saw the photo, I did think there was a resemblance—they both use cubes as a compositional form. But when I saw the original, it became clear that this is entirely different. Chuck Close fills his grids with various colors, relying on visual blending to create an overall impression. Especially after 2014, his monochromatic cube style was innovative, but this artist's work takes an entirely distinct path."

He gestured toward the painting, his eyes filled with admiration. "The cubes in this work aren't just about filling spaces with color—they're like a form of wordless calligraphy. Each stroke carries the spiritual essence of Eastern calligraphy, imbued with the minimalist spirit of Zen. I've never encountered a painting language like this. It's stripped to its bare essentials, yet it gives color the most profound and unfiltered expression. It isn't about technique—it's about innovation."

The room grew quiet as everyone listened intently. Jonathan continued, "The most challenging thing in art is breaking through existing languages. Across millennia, countless artists have tried, but only a handful have succeeded. Jackson Pollock is a prime example. Even though many try to mimic him, none have come close to his impact."

He paused, took a deep breath, and looked resolute. "The essence of art lies in creation. The first words of the Bible are, 'In the beginning, God created,' and that's where artists are closest to divinity. If this artist had begun exploring the visual language before 2014, he would undoubtedly have been an originator—a true pioneer. That level of innovation places him on par with the great masters of art."

Jonathan's words left everyone in awe, underscoring why he was such a pivotal figure at the Metropolitan Museum of Art.

He added, "A museum's mission is to document and present art history. We must identify and safeguard groundbreaking artistic languages and artists. Missing out on work like this means missing a chapter in the evolution of art history. It's like a museum without a Jackson Pollock—it's hard to call it world-class."

Jonathan hesitated, his voice lowering as he added, "To be honest, this painting undoubtedly belongs in a museum. The only issue is..." His voice trailed off, leaving an air of mystery.

Julia leaned closer, unable to hide her curiosity. "The only issue is what?"

Jonathan fell silent for a moment before shaking his head gently. "There's just so much about its story that remains unclear."

Molly interjected, "I don't care about all your highbrow art talk. Art is simple for me—I either like it or don't. And I like this painting. I understand why Lisha loved it enough to buy it—it reminds me of my mother when she was young."

As Molly spoke, she pulled out her phone and showed everyone a photo of her mother, Aliza, from her youth. The image displayed a breathtakingly elegant young woman in a white ballet dress. Aliza's large eyes, high cheekbones, and sculpted lips bore an uncanny resemblance to Marilyn Monroe. Though she appeared to be only 17 or 18, her mature demeanor gave her an aura of timeless elegance.

Molly added, "This photo was taken in 1940s Shanghai, just after she graduated high school. Her family consisted of Russian-Jewish refugees who had ended up in Shanghai in the 1920s or 30s. She grew up in Shanghai, attended a French school, spoke fluent French, and loved painting and ballet. Later, she married my father and chose to stay in Shanghai."

Julia asked curiously, "And then?"

Lisha replied, "Her family left Shanghai in 1952 and eventually settled in New York. But my grandmother stayed behind for my grandfather's sake, and they were separated from her family forever. Molly and I both admire this painting of Mailyn Monroe because it reveals her inner emotional struggles. Beneath the beauty, there's an unspeakable sadness and solitude, much like my grandmother's photo—it reflects a sense of bewilderment at the turning points of history. Not all artworks manage to convey such depth of emotion."

Jonathan commented, "I'd love to meet this artist and hear about his creative motivation. A great artwork always inspires curiosity about the story behind it."

Molly laughed and teased, "Then you're asking the right person! The old master said that the collector of this painting should already know, as the energy of his creation is conveyed through the work itself!"

Jonathan and James chuckled, finding her words amusing.

Lisha didn't respond but seriously asked Jonathan, "I think this painting could belong in the MET."

Jonathan thought momentarily and said, "From technique, form, and color, this painting is museum-worthy. However, to get into the MET, the artist needs a certain level of fame and recognition. The MET typically accepts works donated by prominent collectors or institutions, which can take years."

Lisha replied sarcastically, "The MET operates on elitist principles—fame or fortune is a must."

Jonathan raised his hands helplessly. "There's not much I can do about that."

Lisha smiled and said, "Then maybe we should change the game. Why should we keep playing by the rules when we could rewrite them?"

At that moment, Lisha resolved to find a way to get the painting into the MET, even if it was an uphill battle. But she knew it would be risky and didn't want to drag Jonathan and James into it. Torn between her determination and concern for her friends, she decided to confide in James first to gauge his willingness to take a risk.

Jonathan asked, "Do you have a plan?"

Lisha smiled and shook her head. "I have a few ideas. Let me discuss them with James first."

Julia interjected, "Whatever it is, count me in for the fun!"

The gathering was a success. Everyone Lisha had hoped to invite was there, and they all loved the painting she had purchased. For Lisha, that was a tremendous comfort. The next step was figuring out how to sneak the painting into the MET. She walked into the kitchen, opened another bottle of wine, and called out to the guests in the living room, "Everyone, come have more wine!"

Molly glanced at her and whispered, "Are you drunk?"

"Not at all!" Lisha replied with a grin. "I'm just thrilled with how great this evening turned out. It's helped me make up my mind!"

From the kitchen, she looked out at the lively crowd in the living room, chatting and laughing under the bright lights. Above their heads, the painting of Mailyn Monroe seemed to smile warmly at the guests as if joining in the festivities.

Beyond the living room windows, Manhattan's skyline shimmered in the night.

Chapter V. **The Cost of Adventure**

Jonathan Walton

Outside the Metropolitan Museum of Art, Manhattan bustled with the constant flow of people and traffic. James walked past a street musician playing the guitar. The melodic sound drifted through the lively cityscape, its distinctly Eastern undertone subtly contrasting the urban surroundings. The exotic charm of the music captivated passersby, drawing their attention to the musician.

This street musician would occasionally appear here to play his guitar; every time he did, a crowd of tourists would inevitably gather around. James couldn't help but recall something Lisha had said the last time they walked by: "An electric guitar producing the resonance of a guzheng—it's like the flowing waters of Jiangnan. Only in New York could you find such talent!"

With this thought in mind, James paused. After the musician finished a piece, James approached the musician and placed a five-dollar bill into the guitar case. The musician nodded in gratitude, his warm smile leaving James with a pleasant sense of comfort.

James continued into the MET, weaving through clusters of people gathered around its famous paintings. He stopped momentarily, observing as some visitors raised their phones to snap pictures while others took selfies in front of the iconic works of art.

Lisha's words echoed in his mind, "I still believe that my Marilyn Monroe painting, if placed in the MET, would be equally admired. Sure, the MET's reputation lends any artist and artwork an extraordinary aura, but '*The Last Marilyn Monroe*' is exceptional. It just needs to be showcased for everyone to appreciate."

A bold idea flashed through James's mind, and he was startled by the audacity of his own thoughts.

Maybe it was Lisha's seed planting. Perhaps it was sheer impulsiveness. But he suddenly thought of a plan to get *The Last Marilyn Monroe* into the museum.

Without hesitation, he made his way to Jonathan's office.

"Hey, buddy," James gestured with a familiar hand sign and said to Jonathan, who was on a phone call. Lunch is on me today."

Still on the call, Jonathan glanced up, saw James, and nodded with a smile, signaling his agreement.

Jonathan was five years older than James and came from a

traditional artistic family. His parents owned a prestigious gallery in Manhattan and had high hopes for him, expecting him to inherit the family business. However, Jonathan's rebellious nature made him resist their plans. He disliked the commercialized operations of the gallery and the behind-the-scenes manipulations that propelled artists or artworks to fame, yearning instead to escape the so-called art world.

During middle school, Jonathan's father had an affair, leading to a tumultuous divorce that dragged on for years. This fractured marriage left Jonathan bitterly disillusioned during his formative years. By the time he reached senior high school, the weight of his parents' split crushed his dreams, and he began contemplating running away. Upon graduating, Jonathan boldly decided to leave America and travel to Europe to carve out his path.

In France, he joined a fledgling arts startup as a curatorial assistant. He soon entered a relationship with his boss, a French curator, and moved into her Parisian home. Initially, this chapter of his life felt liberating, allowing him to distance himself from his New York upbringing. However, cracks began to form in their relationship. His girlfriend's dominance—both in work and personal life—left Jonathan feeling trapped, as though he had exchanged one set of controlling parents for another. This realization sparked an internal struggle, pushing him toward independence. During this period, Jonathan unexpectedly began to empathize with his father. Perhaps his father had felt similarly stifled by his mother's strong personality, leading him to seek solace elsewhere. This epiphany prompted Jonathan to reevaluate his relationships with his parents and reassess his future.

Determined to make a change, Jonathan secretly applied to Yale University, the same institution his parents had attended. When he received his acceptance letter, he returned to New York without looking back.

Jonathan's parents were overjoyed at his return. They supported him by covering his tuition fees, allowing him to focus entirely on his studies. At Yale, Jonathan encountered two people who would profoundly impact his life. The first was Julia, an impassioned art columnist he met at an art talk hosted by his parents' gallery. Julia's independent insights into art deeply resonated with Jonathan, inspiring him to realign his life's direction and reenter the art world. After two years of foundational courses, Jonathan declared his major in art history, starting anew.

The second person was James. The two met at Yale and became fast friends. James's humor and warmth gave Jonathan a sense of ease he hadn't felt in years, while Jonathan's experience and artistic perspectives earned James's admiration. Their friendship quickly deepened.

While Jonathan pursued art history, James focused on market management. After graduation, James became an administrative assistant to the director of contemporary art at the Metropolitan Museum of Art. On the other hand, Jonathan briefly returned to his father's gallery. When James noticed a job opening in his department for someone with a background in art history, he immediately recommended Jonathan. It led to the two friends reuniting at the same institution, sharing daily lunches and discussing life and work.

Jonathan's strong artistic background and exceptional organizational skills quickly garnered recognition at the MET. He was soon promoted to senior assistant to the director of the Contemporary Art Curatorial Department, where he managed various responsibilities. James was his best man when Jonathan married Julia, witnessing his friend's journey into marital bliss.

Brothers' Bond

At noon, James and Jonathan arrived at a bustling restaurant near the Metropolitan Museum of Art. As they waited for a table outside, they were already deep in animated conversation. Once seated by a window inside, with sunlight streaming in, James excitedly continued discussing Lisha. A waiter in a white shirt and black apron placed a bottle of Pellegrino on the table next to their neatly arranged silverware. The restaurant buzzed with activity, filled with chatter and the clinking of cutlery, while waitstaff weaved seamlessly through the crowd. The sparkling bubbles in the Pellegrino rose steadily, mirroring James's spirited demeanor as he discussed his ambitious plan to help Lisha get *The Last Marilyn Monroe* displayed in the museum. Meanwhile, Jonathan fiddled with his napkin, his brows furrowed in thought.

James had heard that an upcoming contemporary art exhibition at the museum, curated and managed by Jonathan's department, was in the works. To him, this seemed like the perfect opportunity.

"This exhibition is a godsend!" James said excitedly. "We could sneak *The Last Marilyn Monroe* into the display during the setup. We can put it somewhere inconspicuous—maybe no one will notice!"

Jonathan paused before speaking, his tone calm but firm. "James, this isn't a trivial matter. If we're caught, both of us could be fired, and our careers would be over. Worse, we might never work in this field again."

James waved off the concern. "There are so many artworks in the museum every day. Who would even notice one new painting? This piece deserves to be seen by the public. Besides, it would only be for a few days. What could go wrong?"

Jonathan shook his head, his voice growing more serious. "It's not about whether someone notices—it's about you even daring to think of something like this. You've changed, James. You care about Lisha but can't let her lead you by the nose. She's capable and accomplished—do you think she needs you to do this to prove herself?"

Jonathan had noticed a transformation in James ever since he met Lisha. Over the years, James had dated countless women but never entertained the idea of settling down. He often dismissed the notion of marriage with a casual "I'm just not ready to commit." But everything changed when he met Lisha last year. He fell for her instantly and began pursuing her with fervor. However, Lisha maintained a certain emotional distance despite James's evident passion. Although she agreed to be his girlfriend, she didn't seem to reciprocate his intensity.

James often confided his confusion and frustrations to Jonathan, his closest friend and trusted confidant. Jonathan adored Lisha. Her unique perspectives on art and her insightful commentary always left a deep impression on him. However, as an observer, he couldn't ignore the stark differences between Lisha and James.

Lisha was shaped by adversity—a first-generation immigrant who had to build her life in New York from scratch, relying solely on her grit and determination. Her ambition and resilience were evident. In contrast, James had grown up in the affluent suburbs of New York, leading a comfortable and carefree life, shielded from any significant hardships. He had never indeed fought for anything.

Jonathan had tried to make James see the disparity. "Lisha isn't like you, James. She's someone who had to fight for everything she has. If you want to be with her, you'll have to show her that you're willing to make sacrifices for her and take a gamble."

Jonathan's words hit James hard, resonating deeply within him. He realized his love for Lisha wasn't just about infatuation with a beautiful woman. It was something far more profound, a stirring in his soul that he couldn't ignore. Though he had never believed in fate, meeting Lisha made him question everything. He felt an inexplicable connection with her that spanned beyond the surface.

Now, hearing Jonathan's unspoken doubts, James defended himself. "Lisha and I are connected by more than this painting. Her family and mine share a history rooted in Shanghai. Think about it—two descendants from different worlds, crossing continents to meet and connect in New York. Don't you think it's destiny's way of reuniting two distant histories through us? Shanghai is more than just a city from our ancestors' memories. It's a symbol, a bond, hiding secrets that link us. Honestly, this painting holds immense significance for her. It represents her grandmother, her heritage, and her belief in what contemporary art should be. She's only asking to put it in the museum for a few days. How can I stand by and do nothing?"

Jonathan sighed, "Look, man, I get it. But honestly, she's not even your wife yet. Why are you going to such lengths?"

James suddenly declared, "She will be my wife. She's the love of my life. And if you help me sneak this painting into the MET, I'll propose to her right before it."

Jonathan was stunned, "Propose? Wow, James, you're serious. No wonder you're so reckless—driven by love, I see!"

James nodded earnestly, "Exactly. I want her to know that her dreams are my dreams. She deserves my support, and I'm willing to give it."

Jonathan felt a surge of understanding. Knowing how deeply personal and transformative love can be, he could relate to James's feelings. Their bond went beyond Yale and the museum—rooted in their shared experience of New York City. Jonathan had grown up on Manhattan's Upper East Side, near his parents' prestigious gallery, while James was raised in the affluent Westchester suburbs. Both were deeply connected to Manhattan as their home and shared an emotional anchor.

Moreover, Jonathan realized the intertwining of their fates. If Shanghai had been the city that connected James's grandfather and Lisha's grandmother, then New York was the city that had brought James and Lisha together, tying three disparate lives into a single narrative. Perhaps it was fate's hand that brought them all here.

Jonathan knew that without his help, James would struggle to pull off this plan. And now, seeing James's determination and willingness to take risks for love, Jonathan couldn't stand idly by.

"Alright," Jonathan finally said with a sigh. "You've set your mind on this, aren't you? I can't let you do it alone."

James's face lit up, "You'll help me? Thank you, Jonathan—you're a lifesaver!"

Jonathan shook his head, his voice cautious. "But let me warn you—this plan is perilous. If anything goes wrong, we're toast. Losing our jobs is just the beginning. If this blows up, we'll face consequences we might not be ready for. Are you prepared to handle that?"

James nodded resolutely. He understood the gravity of their plans but knew there was no turning back. It wasn't just about earning Lisha's love; it was about showing her that he would stand by her dreams as her lifelong partner, no matter the cost.

Getting Ready

After several days of careful consideration, Jonathan realized there might be a feasible way to get *The Last Marilyn Monroe* into the museum.

Currently, all the museum collections were stored in the underground collection vault. The key was figuring out how to get *The Last Marilyn Monroe* into the vault. Once it was there, the installation team would move the artwork to its designated location in the gallery during setup. Jonathan handled the inventory and numbering of these pieces daily, so he was intimately familiar with the entire process. If the painting reached the vault, the rest would be smooth sailing. The challenge lay in how to transport it. Several freight elevators connected the underground collection vault to the museum's first floor, and a single security officer guarded the first floor's rear entrance on rotating shifts. Once past the rear entrance, it was moved through a corridor and into the freight elevator—an area without human security but monitored by 24-hour surveillance cameras linked to the control room.

Jonathan remembered his childhood friend, William Gold, who was incredibly resourceful. If anyone could figure out a way to get the painting into the vault, it was William.

Jonathan planned to have William deliver the painting and arrange for someone to temporarily disable the museum's infrared monitoring system. That would allow them to transport the painting into the vault undetected. One key part of the plan was Jonathan's relationship with Lee, one of the security guards stationed at the rear entrance. Lee, an experienced and well-respected guard in his 60s, had worked at the MET for over a decade and was in the process of retiring. His colleagues often followed his lead, so having him on their side was crucial.

Jonathan invited Lee over for drinks at his apartment to ensure his cooperation. Lee was a trusted confidant, and Jonathan had gotten him the job at the museum years ago. Over a few glasses of whiskey, Jonathan laid out his request.

"Lee, I need a favor. A piece must be brought into the museum's collection vault, but it's currently outside. I was hoping you could help us out."

Lee, who was already a little tipsy, thumped his chest confidently. "Jonathan, for you, no problem! Consider it done."

"Have you finalized your retirement papers?" Jonathan asked casually.

"Yup, all done. Next week's my last week at the MET."

Jonathan's heart sank slightly. He realized the clock was ticking—if they were going to pull this off, it had to happen next week before Lee retired. After that, the plan would become much more challenging to execute.

Willian Gold, The Key Player

Coincidences often play a pivotal role in achieving greatness, embodying the Chinese philosophy of "heaven's timing, earth's conditions, and human harmony."

When Jonathan thought of asking his buddy William Gold for help, Lisha and Molly were talking about him, too. They were deliberating on how to find someone to transport *The Last Marilyn Monroe* to the backdoor of the museum. Lisha initially proposed hiring a private moving company to deliver the painting to the museum's rear entrance discreetly. However, Molly vehemently objected: "Absolutely not! The fewer people who know about this, the better! We need William Gold. He's a professional and can ensure everything goes off without a hitch. Besides, we'll probably need his technician, Leo."

Molly's fiancé, William Gold, was an American with a Chinese name. A former Marine, he later attended law school, passed the bar exam, and started as a junior associate at a prominent Manhattan law firm. But William soon realized that the repetitive paperwork and courtroom debates of legal practice failed to bring him true fulfillment. A few years later, he quit his job and opened a private investigation firm. Leveraging his sharp instincts, military training, and extensive social network, William solved countless cases for diverse clients.

William excelled at navigating complex problems and building connections. He could effortlessly adapt when dealing with billionaires, artists, or street vendors. He was skilled in surveillance systems, disguises, and rapid emergency response. His signature motto was, "No problem is unsolvable with the right strategy."

For William, this mission was "child's play." He understood that the real challenge wasn't physically moving the painting into the museum but bypassing its sophisticated security systems. After reviewing the museum's floor plan and security protocols provided by Jonathan, he confidently declared, "I can handle this. The key is to stay calm. If anything goes wrong, no one panics."

The night before the operation, William gathered his team at his detective office and unveiled their gear: fake truck logos, custom transport straps, and infrared interference devices. He meticulously walked the team through each step of the plan and contingency measures, inspiring confidence in everyone present.

William's most trusted ally was Leo, his brilliant technician. Leo had hacked into the museum's surveillance system, embedding an invisible bug that could replace live footage with pre-recorded blank feeds. He also prepared a portable infrared jammer for emergencies.

"The monitoring and infrared systems are covered," Leo reassured William. "As long as we stick to the plan, no one will notice a thing."

That night, the team gathered at Lisha's apartment. A detailed museum floor plan on the kitchen table was spread out, marked with gallery locations, camera placements, and infrared sensor zones.

Jonathan circled critical areas with a pen: "We'll enter through the rear door, follow this corridor, and head straight to the collection vault. This is our route. From 2 to 3 a.m., the infrared sensors undergo a self-check. It is our only window."

William furrowed his brow slightly. "One hour for the entire operation? Is that enough time?"

Leo nodded confidently, "Technically, it's more than enough. If we stick to the schedule, we'll be in and out in under 15 minutes."

Lisha and James leaned over the intricate map, visibly tense. The magnitude of the plan made them both draw sharp breaths. William, however, remained composed. His military experience and Leo's expertise gave him quiet assurance.

Jonathan muttered, "This is the biggest gamble of my career."

Days earlier, Jonathan repeatedly confirmed with James whether he was fully committed, emphasizing the stakes. If the plan failed, they would lose their jobs and futures in the art business.

James had responded resolutely, "I trust William's capabilities.

He'll get it done!"

William interrupted Jonathan's mutterings: "Time's short. Let's go over the details one more time."

Jonathan reiterated sternly, "Remember, this isn't a game. If we're caught, the consequences will be severe. There's no room for hesitation—everyone must execute the plan flawlessly." He handed William a detailed security protocol.

Leo showcased the portable infrared jammer, "This device disables sensors for five minutes but can only be used once. Timing is everything."

William added, "Once inside the museum, follow the plan to the letter. Any deviation could lead to failure."

Lisha concluded with unwavering conviction, "Everyone, remember, we're not stealing a painting—we're giving a masterpiece a chance to be seen." Her voice was firm, and her eyes glimmered with determination.

Chapter VI. **Night of the Operation**

The "Sneak–In" Success

Night had fallen over the neon-lit streets of Manhattan as a white cargo van crept toward the rear entrance of the Metropolitan Museum of Art. With a decal reading "New York Art Association," the van was faintly lit under the amber streetlights, masking its true purpose.

The van belonged to William Gold's company. That night, William, Leo, and James were brimming with nerves and anticipation. William had meticulously prepared protective equipment for *The Last Marilyn Monroe*. He wrapped the painting in a transparent protective cover and secured it in the van with professional-grade transport straps he'd bought from Home Depot. "Be gentle—don't let the straps scrape the painting," he muttered as he carefully tightened them.

Upon arriving at the designated spot, William unfastened the straps and whispered to James, "Careful, this painting is big and heavy. Don't let it hit the doorframe while we move it."

James stood by the rear entrance, tension etched across his face. He could almost hear his heart pounding.

William turned to Leo and said, "We can't stay here long. If someone shows up, we're in trouble. Let's move quickly." Then, he instructed James, "Stay in the car. If anyone comes, drive around the block and come back."

James nodded, slipping into the driver's seat. His nerves were taut as he imagined himself as a character in an action movie. The adrenaline coursing through him was almost palpable.

"The surveillance has been switched, and the infrared interference device is activated. We have a 15-minute window," Leo said from inside the car, monitoring the museum's live feed. The cameras on the screen showed everything was functioning normally.

The team moved quickly. Just then, the rear door creaked open, startling everyone. It was Lee, arriving right on time. He whispered to James, "The storage area is prepped. Jonathan's got everything lined up—don't waste time."

"Gear check," William ordered. "Move fast, but stay calm."

The team quickly inspected their equipment, which included infrared jammers, a portable dolly, and a toolkit. *The Last Marilyn Monroe* was then carefully placed on the custom dolly.

Jonathan wore a discreet earpiece inside the museum, whispering updates to the team. "The guards just switched shifts. We've got a ten-minute window. Everything's clear."

Once inside the rear entrance, the team reached a zone guarded by infrared sensors. Leo pulled out his handheld device to turn off the infrared grid. A small screen displayed the sensor network as he carefully neutralized the specific zones.

"Four, three, two, one—go!" Leo counted down in a hushed voice. The team quickly crossed the blind spot and proceeded toward the storage room.

Suddenly, Leo's jammer flickered. He frowned at his screen, his fingers flying across the keyboard. "Small hiccup. Hold on." After a few tense moments, the grid dimmed again. "Fixed," he murmured confidently.

The museum was eerily silent except for a faint hum in the air and the gentle whir of security cameras. Jonathan led the way to the storage room and swiped his keycard at the door. The lock hesitated momentarily, his palms damp with sweat as he held his breath. With a soft "beep," the door unlocked, and the team slipped inside.

After positioning the painting in the storage room, Jonathan whispered, "They'll start setting up tomorrow. If no one scrutinizes the inventory, the painting will blend in." William nodded. "Let's get out of here. Leave no trace."

On their way out, faint footsteps and the crackle of a walkie-talkie echoed in the distance. William gestured for the team to hide.

Pressed against the wall, they held their breath as a security guard passed, oblivious. Leo whispered, "All clear—move."

Minutes later, they exited the museum and returned to the van. William drove away smoothly, navigating the city streets with practiced ease. After a few cubes, he dropped James off near a subway station, advising him to head home inconspicuously before driving off to dispose of any evidence.

James lingered at the subway entrance, glancing back at the van disappearing into the city's glow. A chilly breeze swept past, making him shiver. He ducked into the subway station, the neon reflections on his face flickering between excitement and apprehension.

Love Conquers All

William returned to his office and found Molly waiting anxiously. He told her the painting had been successfully delivered to the Metropolitan Museum of Art. Molly was so excited that she rushed forward to kiss him, then immediately picked up her phone to call Lisha.

William stopped her, saying, "Relax, James will tell her himself."

Later that night, Lisha was at home when James arrived unannounced.

As soon as James entered, he collapsed onto the couch in the living room, exhausted as if he had just run a marathon.

Seeing Lisha bring him hot tea, James weakly said, "I was so nervous, but the mission is accomplished."

Lisha hugged James tightly, her voice trembling with emotion as she said, "You must have been so nervous. I can only imagine."

James held her and said, "For you, it was all worth it."

Lisha never imagined that James would indeed take a risk for her. Although she liked James, she had always felt unsatisfied with his overly cautious and rule-following nature. She admired men who dared to challenge the status quo and take risks. To her, the ideal partner was someone whose thoughts and actions could surpass hers, someone who could inspire and push her forward.

During her university years in China, Lisha had no shortage of admirers, but her focus on studying abroad left her less interested in serious relationships. After moving to New York, her tall figure and unique exotic charm quickly made her the center of attention, attracting numerous suitors. She went on a few dates but never found anyone who made her heart race.

James stood out as the most genuine and dedicated among all her admirers. His sincerity and persistence touched Lisha, but this was not enough to convince her to consider marriage. To Lisha, marriage required external compatibility and a deep, soulful connection. She firmly believed that the man she would marry had to make her heart skip a beat, not merely a well-qualified man who left her feeling uncertain.

However, at this moment, Lisha saw James in a completely different light. The man before her was no longer the polite and methodical professional she once knew. If the James of the past had been a supporting character in her story, he had now transformed into the protagonist. Lisha's feelings shifted subtly yet profoundly, and her gaze at James carried a warmth and complexity that had never been there before. Perhaps, unbeknownst to them both, the spark of love had finally been ignited.

Looking directly into James's eyes, Lisha's voice softened with emotion as she said, "Wow, I never expected you'd take such a risk for me. I'm truly moved."

With that, she wrapped her arms around him and kissed him passionately. James was stunned and exhilarated. He never thought that his actions today would earn such a fiery response from Lisha. He knew Lisha had kept a certain distance throughout their year-long relationship, never fully opening her heart to him. As someone experienced in love, James had dated numerous women before and understood the unpredictable nature of relationships. He had always held back, never fully revealing his emotions, fearing the pain of unrequited love. But meeting Lisha had upended all his usual principles and rationality. He pursued her relentlessly, lowering his guard in ways he never had before. Even he couldn't quite explain why—perhaps it was fate.

Falling for Lisha, James finally understood the mix of anticipation and disappointment his former girlfriends must have felt. Reflecting on his past, he couldn't help but feel a pang of guilt for the way he had treated them. Perhaps this was karma, he thought, for making him so powerless in the face of his goddess.

As Lisha, uncharacteristically passionate, embraced and kissed him at that moment, James realized this was a turning point. Gratitude and joy surged within him. He silently thanked the lord as he held her tightly and returned her kiss. In the dim glow of the living room, their silhouettes melded together, becoming one. For that fleeting moment, the world seemed to fade away, leaving only the burning intensity of their love.

The Final Setup

Early the following day, Jonathan arrived at the museum's exhibition space. He watched workers move the selected pieces from the storage area into the gallery. Among the collection was *The Last Marilyn Monroe*.

One mover groaned, "This thing is so heavy! We should've had the sculpture team handle it."

Another nodded, "Yeah, they'd use an indoor crane for something this big."

Jonathan hurried over to intervene, directing the workers to use a cart to wheel the painting to its designated spot. He had previously added the painting's details and location to the inventory list.

During the setup, the sheer volume of work and the tight schedule left no time for questions about the source of each piece. The staff focused solely on ensuring the inventory matched the assigned exhibit numbers.

Inside the gallery, workers in uniforms installed paintings

and sculptures against the tall white walls. Following Jonathan's instructions, the movers placed *The Last Marilyn Monroe* on an unassuming wall in a corner, surrounded by sculptures. Despite its inconspicuous location, the vibrant painting immediately caught the eye, standing out from the surrounding pieces.

"This is interesting. I like it," one of the crew remarked casually. "Feels more captivating than the others."

Jonathan stood by a nearby sculpture, observing the painting. Lisha was right, he thought—the piece was stunning. Even in this secluded corner, its brilliance couldn't be hidden. He studied the painting, his expression a mix of admiration and unease. He muttered under his breath, "This doesn't belong in a corner—it deserves an entire wall in the main gallery."

And so, the painting quietly became part of the museum's collection. As for what would happen next, Jonathan decided to take it one step at a time. For now, he had done his part. The rest was out of his hands.

Chapter VII. **The Birth of an Art Sensation**

In the Spotlight

The following day, before the museum opened, James rushed to where the painting had been placed. He examined it from every angle and couldn't help but feel it stood out too much. It was exceptionally vivid and radiant compared to the surrounding artworks as if it had its own halo.

He quietly told Jonathan, "This piece seemed huge at Lisha's place, but it fits perfectly here. Still, it's so eye-catching. Do you think it'll attract too much attention?"

Jonathan sighed and replied, "There's nothing else we can do. Luckily, there are plenty of other works here by famous artists, so hopefully, it won't draw too much notice. But then again, if it does, it means we've achieved our goal."

After the museum opened, Lisha, Julia, and Molly arrived together, heading for the gallery where the painting was displayed.

"Wow!" The three women stood before *The Last Marilyn Monroe*, unable to hold back their admiration.

Lisha beamed. "I told you—this piece belongs in a museum like this, a temple of art."

Julia agreed, "The larger space here really lets you appreciate it. You can study it from a distance and then up close."

Meanwhile, Molly had already started filming the painting on her phone. She recorded its transformation as she moved closer—from a vivid whole to cubes of color, transitioning from figurative to abstract. Eventually, her screen displayed only bold, vibrant strokes, each cube standing out in remarkable detail.

"Oh, my goodness!" Julia exclaimed. "You've outdone yourself."

At that moment, a small group of tourists gathered nearby, drawn by the painting. One of them exclaimed, "Wow, it's Marilyn Monroe!" Their curiosity piqued, and others ran over, snapping photos and posing for pictures in front of the piece.

As more visitors entered the gallery, the painting quickly became the center of attention. A steady stream of people gathered to admire it, some even taking selfies with it as their backdrop.

Lisha, unable to contain her delight, whispered to Julia and Molly, "See? I knew so many people would love it."

The three women stepped back, crossing their arms as they

watched the growing crowd. Wave after wave of visitors entered the gallery, stopping to admire *The Last Marilyn Monroe*. They posed, snapped pictures, and marveled at the painting's beauty. Soon, a circle of people had formed around it, and no matter how many left, new visitors quickly took their place.

Molly continued filming the scene with her phone. "Next time, I'm bringing my camera," she grins. "This is too entertaining!"

Watching the endless flow of people captivated by the painting, Julia couldn't help but muse aloud, "I should write an article about this piece."

She turned to Molly. "You've got to get your fiancé to track down this artist's address for me. I need to interview him."

Lisha immediately stopped her, "Don't blow this up! Remember, we snuck this painting in here!"

Julia sighed, nodding, "Ugh, there's my journalist instinct kicking in again."

As more visitors crowded around *The Last Marilyn Monroe*, it became clear that this once-hidden piece had become a star attraction, drawing attention as if it were already a masterpiece of great renown.

Overnight Fame

Within days, *The Last Marilyn Monroe* had gone viral. Photos and videos of the painting appeared on social media, sparking an avalanche of shares and reposts.

A week later, its online popularity had exploded, with views and clicks surpassing a million. The unexpected attention quickly drew the interest of local media.

Julia's newspaper editor approached her about the viral painting. "Write a follow-up piece for your column," he said. "This is making waves."

Julia immediately called Lisha. "If I don't write about this, someone else will," she explained. "It's better if I handle it—it'll be fairer to you, me, and the paper."

Alarmed, Lisha contacted James, who rushed to Jonathan to discuss the situation.

The sudden fame of *The Last Marilyn Monroe* caught them off guard. What had begun as a playful act of rebellion—a critique of contemporary art's pretentiousness—was now spiraling into something far beyond their control.

James worried that the painting's potential sensation might lead people to trace its origins, ultimately implicating Jonathan. No matter what, James was prepared to take responsibility for his own decisions and accept the consequences, but he was determined not to drag his best friend into the mess.

On the other hand, Jonathan was anxious that any investigation into the painting could expose his actions. After all, what they had done was a clear violation of the MET's regulations, and if it came to light, he would have to face the fallout alone.

"We just wanted people to see the painting," James muttered, frowning. "Now it's gone viral beyond what we intended."

Jonathan sighed, "The biggest risk is that the media will track the painting's origins. If that happens, it's over for both of us."

James's resolve hardened. "This was my idea. I'll take full responsibility."

On a gloomy Manhattan morning, with rain threatening to fall, Lisha arrived at her office, lost in thought. Before she could settle in, Martin approached her.

"I saw your painting on the news!" Martin said, his piercing blue eyes fixed on her.

Lisha's heart sank. She had deliberately kept Martin in the dark about sneaking the painting into the museum, knowing fewer people involved meant less risk. She had forgotten that Martin had once seen the painting at her apartment.

Caught off guard, Lisha hesitated, her words faltering.

Martin narrowed his eyes, "Wait... did you sneak that painting into the museum?"

Meeting his gaze, Lisha replied firmly, "I hired someone to do it. You know me—I just wanted more people to see this incredible work of art. It was worth it!"

Lisha hated lying but felt she had no choice. She couldn't risk implicating Jonathan or James.

Martin shook his head, "You're far too careless—how could you delegate something like this to someone else?" What if they turn on you? You could get sued and have no defense. You'd better consult a reliable lawyer."

Lisha hesitated, "Let me think about it. If needed, I'll ask William Gold. He used to be a lawyer."

Martin's eyes lit up, "A viral art piece like this has so much potential. We should consider creating an art fund and focusing on pieces like this in the future."

Lisha sighed, "All I wanted was for this painting to be in a museum. I never imagined it would become a selfie hotspot. "It's truly a case of "unintentionally planting willows and seeing them grow into shade! "

While the painting's sudden fame boosted her confidence, Lisha knew her immediate priority was managing the current situation.

What Now?

After work, everyone involved in the plot gathered at James's Williamsburg apartment to discuss their next steps.

Williamsburg, Brooklyn, has transformed from an industrial zone into a thriving arts district. Along the East River, the streets are lined with former factory buildings converted into apartments, vibrant graffiti murals, and towering modern constructions. The Manhattan skyline is visible across the river. Once a haven for artists, Williamsburg has become a favorite neighborhood for Wall Street professionals. With its rising property values, it now rivals Manhattan in desirability.

James' apartment occupies the entire first floor of a converted factory. It is spacious and bright and boasts panoramic views. The evening sun streams through French floor-to-ceiling windows, casting warm orange hues onto the minimalist yet elegant interior. James was among the first wave of young professionals to move into Williamsburg, signing a 20-year lease when property prices were still much lower. Back then, the cost of his expansive floor was comparable to that of a one-bedroom apartment in the area today.

The first time Lisha visited James' home, she was immediately drawn to the artistic vibe of the neighborhood and the breathtaking views. Her impression of James improved instantly. Unlike Manhattan's bustling commercial atmosphere, Brooklyn's charm lay in its unique landscape—an ocean of factory rooftops and water towers reminiscent of the red-tiled roofs of Shanghai's old districts. The rooftops, bathed in sunlight, formed a harmonious interplay of light and shadow, their rhythmic patterns reminiscent of a musical composition.

From James' choice of residence, Lisha could discern his lifestyle and preferences—qualities that resonated with the artistic sensibilities cherished by native New Yorkers.

Tonight, the group gathered around the open kitchen island, stocked with wine, snacks, and salads, while discussing their predicament.

Julia stood by the stove in the kitchen, chatting as Molly prepared a dish.

Molly said, "William managed to track down the artist. He's a painter from southern China who's lived in New York for over thirty years. He rarely participates in the art scene or exhibitions, but there are stories about him. He agreed to a phone interview, though not an in-person one."

"That's fantastic!" Julia exclaimed. "Even a phone interview is a big deal."

Molly hesitated, "Do you think this will cause trouble for James and the others? Once your article is published, the art world will know about this."

Julia smirked, "Maybe it's time they learned what real art looks like. The closed-off, money-driven games of the art world are stifling true talent. This painting could shake things up."

Molly nodded, "I agree with Lisha—this painting deserves to be in a museum for everyone to see. Its reception proves that some of these art rules need changing."

Their conversation grew increasingly animated. They imagined the article might shift the art world's rigid norms.

James, Jonathan, and William gathered over drinks in the living room, brainstorming solutions.

James said, "Maybe we should remove the painting soon to avoid drawing too much attention."

Jonathan shook his head, "That's easier said than done. Getting it in was one thing, but taking it out could be considered theft."

William Gold interjected, "If we got it in, we can get it out the same way."

Jonathan, "Do you think sneaking in and out of the MET is as easy as walking through your front door? Haven't you seen how many people managed to sneak their paintings into the MET, but how many could sneak them back out without getting caught? They all got discovered in the end."

Lisha said anxiously, "I never imagined it would cause such a big mess. I just wanted to display the painting in the MET for a few days so people could see it. It turns out you can never outsmart fate."

Jonathan leaned back, exhaling deeply. "Let's leave it for now and see how things unfold. Sometimes, you just have to trust the universe."

James clasped his hands together. "Let's pray everything works out."

Molly later pulled Lisha aside, "I've been wondering—why go to all this trouble? You're not the artist's agent, and there's no financial gain. Is this about proving something to your dad? Like, even though you're not in the art world anymore, you still have taste?"

Lisha frowned, "Auntie, not everything is about material gain. Art is about spirit and energy. Great art—like Van Gogh or Monet—moves people. It's about the power to touch hearts."

Molly teased, "So you think this painting is Van Gogh reincarnated?"

Lisha's tone turned serious, "They're both high-dimensional artists, but from different eras. Their energy manifests differently. Marilyn

Monroe was an artist, but most people only see her beauty and physicality, missing her emotional depth."

Molly chuckled softly, "I have to admit, James is head over heels for you. He's such a straight-laced guy, yet he pulled this off. I misjudged him before."

Lisha smiled, "I never expected this side of him either. It's exhilarating."

Molly raised an eyebrow. "So, you're in love with him now, huh?"

Lisha laughed, "I just think he's incredibly sexy and worth loving."

Molly quipped, "Seems like men don't need to be super capable—just willing to risk it all for their woman, and they'll win her heart. Your mom will be thrilled to hear this."

Lisha's smile faded, "Auntie, this has to stay between us. No one else can know."

The group gathered for dinner as Molly set the dishes on the beautifully arranged dining table, with candles casting a warm glow.

Lisha glanced at the array of dishes and whispered to Jonathan, "Maybe this painting will change the rules."

Jonathan gave a wry smile, "Let's hope so. But breaking the rules always comes at a steep price."

Outside, Brooklyn's night sky stretched over the East River. Across the water, Manhattan's illuminated skyline shimmered in the distance. *The Last Marilyn Monroe* hung quietly on the wall in the museum, drawing in the museum crowds daily. Its future remained uncertain, but its impact was undeniable.

Chapter VIII. **Fate or Destiny**

Julia Steps Up

Early in the morning, Lisha's phone buzzed on the nightstand. Seeing Julia's name on the screen, she quickly answered. Next to her, James was still sound asleep, as if the world outside had nothing to do with him.

Glancing at James, Lisha tiptoed out of bed and into the bathroom.

"Today's paper is out," Julia said excitedly. "I've emailed you the digital version—take a look."

Lisha opened the email and began reading the article. With each line, her heart raced faster. The piece featured *The Last Marilyn Monroe* and a photo of her grandmother, Aliza. Julia had woven Aliza's story into the narrative, connecting history and art through a poignant lens.

"The Last Marilyn Monroe":
A Painting's Mystery and Controversy
By Julia Walton

In recent days, *The Last Marilyn Monroe*, a captivating painting, has taken both the art world and social media by storm. With its unique artistic style and profound emotional resonance, this artwork has mesmerized audiences while igniting debates about the nature of art and its means of dissemination. From its enigmatic creator to its unexpected debut before the public, the story of *The Last Marilyn Monroe* unfolds like an art–world legend, and the intrigue continues to deepen.

A Bold Fusion of Styles

The Last Marilyn Monroe stuns viewers with its distinctive "cube–painting" style. The piece integrates the bold brushstrokes of Chinese calligraphy with the vibrant textures of Western oil painting. Marilyn Monroe's iconic visage emerges as both familiar and hauntingly new. Her radiant smile exudes starlet charm while betraying a deep, complex melancholy. It is a tribute to Mailyn Monroe's short, tragic life and enduring legacy.

Each vibrant cube of color seems to represent a fragment of Mailyn Monroe's life, pieced together to form a cohesive whole. In this way, Mailyn Monroe symbolizes a bygone American golden age and an emblem of contemporary cultural fragmentation. "This painting doesn't just tell Mailyn Monroe's story; it reflects the existential disarray of a generation grappling with meaning in a fractured society," remarked one art critic.

When viewed from a distance, the painting's fragmented style resolves into a photorealistic whole, a visual metaphor for how disjointed individual experiences coalesce into the shared narratives that define our lives.

The Enigmatic Artist

The artist behind *The Last Marilyn Monroe* is an elusive figure, rumored to have immigrated to the U.S. in the 1980s. After a brief rise as an abstract painter, he retreated into a 16—year hiatus before returning with this groundbreaking new style. Combining Chinese calligraphy's philosophical depth with visual traditions' vibrancy, his work has captivated audiences without his appearances.

When declining interviews, the artist simply replied, "If I could fully express my ideas in words, I wouldn't need to paint." This response embodies the Taoist philosophy that informs his work: a transformative journey from perceiving mountains as mountains to seeing them as no longer mountains and ultimately understanding them as mountains once more. His paintings vividly reflect this profound and cyclical view of existence.

A Public Appearance Amid Controversy

The Last Marilyn Monroe made its surprising debut in the gallery halls of a prominent museum. Amid classic masterpieces, its vibrant presence was impossible to ignore, and it quickly became a focal point for museum—goers and critics alike.

Social media exploded with reactions. While some hailed

it as "the most insightful artwork of the 21st century," others drew comparisons to so-called "banana art," questioning the art market's valuation systems.

"This painting forces us to reevaluate the essence of art—not just as an aesthetic or technical feat but as a medium for societal dialogue," said one seasoned art critic.

A Family's Hidden Story

Beyond its visual appeal, *The Last Marilyn Monroe* carries a profoundly personal backstory. It draws inspiration from the life of a 20th-century Jewish émigré from Shanghai. Her family fled Russia's upheavals in the early 20th century and found refuge in Shanghai, where she experienced a life of love, loss, and resilience amid war and displacement.

A source familiar with the artist noted, "The painting extends her unfinished dreams and pays homage to her legacy. " Mailyn Monroe's portrait resonates with this émigré's life—a story fragmented by history yet made whole through memory and art.

Redefining Artistic Norms

The painting's unexpected appearance challenges traditional modes of art presentation and raises broader questions about who determines artistic value: creators, institutions, or the audience.

"In contemporary art, breaking the rules redefines value," remarked an observer. "The appearance of this work is both an experiment and a declaration: art is no longer a static object but an active participant in societal discourse."

A Tribute to Forgotten Souls

The Last Marilyn Monroe transcends its role as a tribute to Mailyn Monroe, becoming a monument to all souls forgotten or silenced by history. Its visual language reminds us that the narrative of history is ongoing, and we are all part of its dialogue.

With *The Last Marilyn Monroe*, art and society engage in a dynamic conversation that challenges conventions, honors resilience, and beckons us to listen more deeply to the untold stories in our midst.

By the time Lisha finished reading, her eyes were brimming with tears. She returned to the bedroom, gently shook James awake, and handed him her phone.

"Read this," she said softly, her voice quivering with emotion.

Caught in the Whirlwind

Jonathan had not anticipated that Julia would publish such an evocative and impassioned article in her column. Over the years, despite being married, the two of them had always maintained independent careers and rarely commented on each other's work.

Julia hadn't told Jonathan about the article before it was published. Although James had mentioned it to him, Jonathan had been too preoccupied with his simmering anxiety over the past few days to dwell on it. On the morning the article was published, Jonathan saw

Julia's column while reading the newspaper during breakfast. He called out to her as she tidied herself up to leave for work, saying, "Your writing is brilliant!"

Julia felt a wave of relief wash over her. "I didn't tell you earlier because I was worried you wouldn't approve," she admitted.

Jonathan said, "At this point, I'm like a dead pig that doesn't fear boiling water. The risks James and I took for that painting make me wonder if I've lost my mind!"

"Oh my," Julia teased, "Only Lisha would come up with something like a dead pig doesn't fear boiling water.' You and James are falling deeper under her spell!"

Jonathan gave a wry smile, "I used to think it was just James who was mesmerized, but now it feels like I've joined him on the same wild ride. Might as well laugh about it!"

Julia approached him and gently reassured him, "You did the right thing. No matter what, you and James accomplished something no one else dared to do. One day, when you look back, you'll see it was worth it."

Jonathan smiled wryly, "Well, no matter what happens, your article is so well-written that it makes the whole ordeal feel worthwhile. I have a hunch that it might propel you into the spotlight and establish you as a renowned art critic."

Julia laughed, "That would be great—I'd never have to write content I don't care about again."

Jonathan added humorously, "If the worst happens and I lose my job, I'll count on you to support both of us."

Julia smiled playfully, "That would be perfect. We could team up, plan projects together, and devote ourselves entirely to the art we love."

The couple locked eyes and embraced. At that moment, they felt that having each other's understanding was the greatest happiness in the world.

Later that morning, Jonathan walked into the museum with unusually light steps, taking the subway to work. As he sat in his office, his supervisor, Old Joe, said, "Jonathan, have you seen Julia's column today? She gave one of our collection pieces a fantastic write-up—what an article!"

Old Joe was full of praise in the office, "I can't believe no one told me we had such a stunning Marilyn Monroe piece in the collection! Amazing!" he exclaimed. Marilyn Monroe, after all, had been a dream icon for countless men. A striking artwork like this was unforgettable to anyone who saw it.

Hearing this, Jonathan felt his heart drop. It was what he had feared precisely: Julia's article had propelled *The Last Marilyn Monroe* to outshine every other piece in the exhibition. Worse, his boss had now taken notice.

Jonathan forced a strained smile and replied, "With so many items in our collection, some are bound to slip under the radar." Indeed, the museum's modern and contemporary art department alone housed tens of thousands of works across various media, and even department staff members often weren't fully aware of everything in the collection.

Old Joe instructed Jonathan to prepare a detailed report on the painting, including its provenance and artistic significance. Jonathan knew this would undoubtedly attract attention from higher-ups, and he felt a sense of impending doom.

Meanwhile, Julia's newspaper received a flood of emails from readers. Many praised her article and expressed admiration for the painting. Others inquired about the piece, eager to learn more. Julia felt a deep fulfillment but couldn't shake a lingering unease. She worried that the article might bring unintended consequences for Lisha and James.

I'm All In

At lunchtime, Jonathan and James, as usual, went to their favorite trendy restaurant near the museum. On the way, they passed by the street musician who often played in front of the museum. James habitually dropped a few bills into the musician's guitar case.

Once seated in the restaurant, Jonathan couldn't help but tell James, "When Old Joe asked me about the painting, my heart nearly stopped. I was terrified he'd figured it out."

James reassured him, "That's just a guilty conscience talking. As long as we stay quiet, no one will ever know."

"Old Joe asked me to write a report," Jonathan muttered, lowering his voice. "Now we're in real trouble."

James frowned thoughtfully, "Maybe we should get the painting out ahead of time?"

"Taking it out is easy, but if the painting disappears, the museum will report it to the police," Jonathan sighed. "How long can we keep this under wraps?"

"Julia's article was just too good," James said wryly. "We were only trying to pull off a prank, but instead, we turned it into a viral sensation."

Jonathan shook his head in resignation, "You can't predict these things. Since it's already spiraled out of control, we'll have to take it one step at a time."

Life has a way of surprising you. Julia's article resonated with many readers, drawing a steady stream of visitors to the museum to see the painting. Meanwhile, several art influencers posted videos sharing their interpretations of the piece. Like a spark igniting a wildfire, news about the painting was ablaze on social media within a week.

Eventually, a senior vice president of the museum's board took notice and called a meeting with Old Joe, Jonathan's boss, to gather details about the painting's origins for a report to the museum director. Old Joe immediately pressed Jonathan to complete his report on the artwork.

"We need to get the painting out right now, or we'll have no way to explain this," Jonathan told James.

The conspirators who had initially smuggled the painting into the museum reconvened at James' apartment to brainstorm.

Molly busily prepared food in the kitchen while Lisha and the others debated their next move in the living room.

William, ever pragmatic, said, "At this point, there's no point overthinking it. We should just use the same method we did to bring it in and get it out."

Jonathan countered, "Even if we manage to get the painting out, the museum will notice and report it missing."

Lisha sneered, "That's rich. When I wanted to donate the painting to the museum, they refused because I'm not a big name and the artist isn't famous. But now, when I want to return it, they're threatening to call the police?"

James explained, "The problem is, the museum doesn't know we smuggled the painting in. They think it's part of their collection. If it goes missing, of course, they'll investigate."

William nodded, "Investigating is a problem for later. Right now, we need to focus on getting the painting out. If we leave it, we'll just get more trapped."

Jonathan sighed, "I don't see any other choice. Let's do it."

Lisha crossed her arms. "The painting is mine. I'd rather step forward and take all the blame, say I hired people to do it."

"Don't you dare say you hired us!" William said, his nerves on edge.

"You can't do that!" James interjected firmly. "If you come forward, we'll all get dragged down with you."

Jonathan let out a deep sigh. "Looks like we'll have to gamble."

Lisha said calmly, "If I take the blame, it'll be to protect you all. I wouldn't implicate anyone else."

James exhaled and said, "Let's get the painting out first. We'll figure out the rest later. Everything's already out of our control."

When Molly finally brought out the dishes, the group had stopped debating.

Molly, puzzled, asked, "So, what's the plan?"

William quickly replied, "Don't worry about it, honey. We'll handle it."

Prepare for the Worst

That evening, after everyone else had left, James turned to Lisha and said, "I didn't expect this painting to go viral. Now, we're in real trouble."

Lisha, on the other hand, seemed surprisingly calm. As she prepared to brush her teeth, she replied, "Going viral just proves I wasn't wrong—this painting truly deserves to be in a museum. Honestly, I couldn't be happier about that."

James sighed, "Let's just hope we can get the painting out as smoothly as last time."

Lisha walked over and hugged him. "James, you've already done so much for me. I won't let you take the fall if anything goes wrong."

James smiled faintly. "Don't be silly. We're in this together—sink or swim."

Her expression softened, and she rested her head gently on his chest. "Thank you, James."

As Lisha went into the bathroom to shower, James lay on the bed, staring at the ceiling, lost in thought. It was, without a doubt, the most reckless thing he'd ever done. It was as if James, who once lived a quiet, uneventful life working at the museum, had vanished. In his place was a man willing to risk everything for the woman he loved. The transformation was so drastic that he barely recognized himself. But, as the saying goes, no pain, no gain. He had made his choice and prepared to face the consequences.

In the shower, Lisha was also deep in thought. She knew she had dragged James and Jonathan into a risky situation while pursuing her dream. The weight of their loyalty and sacrifices was something she could never repay. Lisha resolved that, no matter what, she would step forward and take full responsibility if things went south. With that decision made, a strange calm washed over her, and her previously racing heart began to settle.

As the city lights glittered brightly over Manhattan, Lisha felt a rare clarity. She understood this was a risk she had to take, and she knew this painting's fate would inevitably alter the course of her life.

Back to Long Island

After leaving James's apartment, Molly and William drove back to their home in Long Island. The car ride was quiet, except for guitar music's gentle strumming through the speakers. A few days earlier, Lisha had sent Molly a link to the street musician's YouTube channel. Molly fell in love with the melodies, which evoked memories of her long-lost childhood in southern China. Since then, the music has become her go-to soundtrack for drives.

Breaking the silence, William remarked, "I've got to say, what Lisha's pulling off here would easily cost thousands of dollars if done professionally."

Molly opened her eyes, startled, "What do you mean? Are you suggesting we charge her?"

William smirked, "Not at all. I just want you to realize how risky this is. Running a business in New York is expensive, and if anything goes wrong, it's not just money—we're talking reputation, too."

Molly, slightly annoyed, retorted, "You sound like you're already anticipating something going wrong."

William, his tone more serious, replied, "I can't help but think Lisha's being a bit naive. All this trouble for one painting—what's the point? Challenging people's perceptions of art? It's a noble idea but incredibly idealistic. His love for Lisha drives James, but Jonathan? He's risking his career and maybe even legal action from the museum. As for me, the only reason I'm involved is because of you."

Molly's initial irritation melted into worry as she listened. "Do you think the risks are higher with taking the painting out?"

"Absolutely," William said firmly. "Sneaking a painting into a museum is one thing. Taking it out? That's theft. If we ever get caught, we'd be treated as criminals."

Molly sighed, reflecting on Jonathan's earlier comments about leaving things in God's hands. "So, what now? Do we rely on divine intervention?"

William responded with a dry chuckle. "God helps those who help themselves. We have to act first. The rest is up to fate."

Molly leaned back, looking out the window. "I still support Lisha. Artists have it so hard, so look at The old master. If no one buys his work, how does he survive? Galleries prioritize young artists for profit, leaving older, more talented ones to fend for themselves. Lisha has always wanted to make a difference in the world. "If everyone only thinks about personal gain, this world will only get worse."

William nodded, "You and Lisha are cut from the same cloth—always thinking on a higher plane. It's why I joined the Marines. I wanted to serve something bigger than myself. Sure, it paid for my college and law degree, but being a lawyer wasn't my dream. Solving problems and helping people—that's my true calling."

Molly smiled softly, "And that's why I fell for you—your idealism."

"Thanks to you, I'm reminded that survival isn't the goal. Making a difference is." William reached over, taking Molly's hand. Trying to lighten the mood, he added, "Don't worry. We got the painting in, and we'll get it out."

Molly chuckled but then said quietly, "I've lived in the U.S. for years, but I still dread breaking the law. At least now I'm a citizen—I don't have to fear losing my green card."

William laughed, "You're my wife—anyone who dares to revoke your status will have to deal with me."

Molly couldn't help but smile. Her heart warmed. As the guitar music filled the car, her thoughts drifted.

In all her years in New York, through a marriage, a divorce, and countless relationships, no one had ever made her feel as secure as William. Though much younger than her, his life experiences had shaped him into a man whose inner strength matched his commanding presence.

On the highway, the lights outside the car window sparkled like stars, and the Manhattan skyline in the distance began to fade further and further away.

Chapter IX. **Another Risky Venture**

A Daring Night

The stillness of New York's museum night was broken by heavy footsteps echoing through its halls. A group of shadowy figures carefully carried a heavy object. Suddenly, an ear-piercing alarm shattered the silence, its shrill sound reverberating through the building. Startled, the group froze, their faces unseen in the dim light but their panic palpable.

"Damn it!" Lee muttered, his voice tense. As the museum's security guard, his instincts kicked in. He let go of his hold, causing the person beside him to stumble as the weight of the painting pulled them off balance.

"What the hell!" the person spat angrily. The faint glow revealed his face—it was James, the assistant director of the museum's exhibition department.

"We must have tripped the infrared sensor!" someone whispered.

The group exchanged frantic glances, their expressions betraying their fear and confusion. A meticulously planned operation, one they thought was foolproof, had gone wrong. Each person looked as if they'd been caught red-handed.

The tension was suffocating. A chaotic, thunderous soundtrack seemed to play on a loop in James's mind. Sweat poured from his body as he stood frozen, paralyzed by fear.

"James! Wake up!" A voice cut through the imaginary cacophony, pulling him back to reality. He blinked and found himself staring at Lisha's concerned face.

James rubbed his eyes, disoriented.

"You were yelling in your sleep," Lisha said, "I woke up and saw you thrashing around. I had to shake you awake."

James sighed, the lingering images of the dream still vivid. "It felt so real," he said, recounting the nightmare to her.

Lisha smiled reassuringly, "You've been under too much stress these past few days. It's no wonder you're having nightmares."

James leaned back, thoughtful, "Didn't you say dreams reflect things about to happen or things our souls have already experienced?"

Lisha laughed lightly, "Do you think you're living in Inception? Stop overthinking it, and get ready. Today's the day we move the painting."

James nodded. He and Jonathan had arranged to remove *The Last Marilyn Monroe* early in the morning before the museum opened. Checking his watch, he saw it was only 3 a.m., giving him a sense of momentary relief.

He quickly headed to the bathroom to shower and dress, preparing for what was likely the riskiest operation they'd undertaken yet. But the nightmare had left a residue of unease in his heart. This final move was their most critical and dangerous action yet.

Mission Failed

The Metropolitan Museum lay silent in the night, its vast halls cloaked in stillness. Suddenly, heavy footsteps echoed through the quiet, accompanied by the cautious movements of several shadowy figures carrying a heavy object. Out of nowhere, the piercing wail of an alarm shattered the silence, reverberating through the museum with a deafening intensity.

The group, startled mid-action, froze in their tracks. Though the dim light obscured their faces, their hesitation was palpable, their movements betraying a moment of panic and uncertainty as the blaring alarm filled the air.

On the surveillance monitors, three shadows moved stealthily, pushing a cart. William led the group, his steps light and his sharp gaze scanning for irregularities. Jonathan and James followed closely, their anxious faces and stiff movements betraying their unease.

"Hold up," Leo's calm voice came through the earpieces. "The camera ahead will pan right. Three seconds to move—stay sharp."

The trio maneuvered carefully, bypassing infrared sensors and slipping past blind spots under Leo's guidance. Everything proceeded smoothly as they reached the display holding *The Last Marilyn Monroe*. Standing before the artwork, they prepared to remove it from the wall.

William suddenly froze, noticing a faint light flickering behind the frame. "Stop!" he whispered sharply.

Jonathan's hand hovered mid-air. "What is it?"

"There's something behind the frame," William said, leaning closer. "It's an RFID sensor."

"What's an RFID sensor?" James asked, whispering nervously.

"A radio frequency identification system," William explained tersely. "It's used to track, monitor, and control items." He immediately asked Leo for advice.

"If they've installed an RFID," Leo replied, "there's no way we can disable it remotely. You'll have to abandon the mission."

William sighed, "We're calling it off."

Jonathan attempted a strained laugh. "What do we need now, Tom Cruise or the Ocean's Eleven crew?"

"Really?" James hissed in frustration. "We're in deep trouble, and you're joking?"

Jonathan shrugged helplessly. "It's how I handle nerves. Without it, I'd be frozen stiff by now!"

James, visibly shaken, muttered, "I need a restroom break."

William gritted his teeth in frustration. Amateurs, he thought. Never again.

Turning to Leo, he said, "We're pulling out. Guide us out safely."

Leo's voice remained steady. "Retrace your path. Move cautiously but quickly."

The trio began their retreat by pushing the cart. As they rounded a corner, the cart's metal edge grazed a wall-mounted sensor.

An ear-piercing alarm shattered the silence.

"Move now!" Leo barked through the earpiece.

Panic-stricken, the team abandoned the cart and bolted toward their entry point. Within moments, the building's exits were locked down.

"The doors are sealed!" William hissed. "Leo, what now?"

"North stairs, second-floor emergency exit," Leo instructed. "Time is tight—go!"

The group sprinted toward the staircase, their footsteps echoing loudly in the empty museum. Red alarm lights swirled above them, heightening the tension.

"Guards approaching from the east!" Leo warned. "You've got a ten-second window. Move faster!"

The trio's breaths came in gasps as they reached the stairwell, only to hear approaching footsteps from another staircase.

"Guards!" Jonathan whispered, his voice tinged with fear.

"Hide!" William commanded, pulling them into a dark storage room.

The air inside was heavy with tension. The guards' footsteps grew louder, and faint voices from their radios filtered through the door: "Suspects may be nearby. Stay alert!"

James trembled, his forehead slick with sweat. "We're doomed..."

"Quiet!" William hissed.

A sudden clatter broke the silence—James had accidentally knocked over a metal shelf.

Outside, the guards stopped. Flashlight beams swept across the room's edges.

William gestured for silence, his hand clenched tightly.

After a tense moment, the guards moved on, distracted by a call.

"Clear," Leo said through the earpiece. "Proceed to the second service elevator—quickly!"

The trio navigated the corridors, following Leo's directions. Finally, they reached the elevator just as distant voices and heavy footsteps signaled the guards' return.

The elevator doors closed, shutting out the chaos. Jonathan and James slumped against the walls, gasping for breath.

When they reached the ground floor, they slipped through the rear exit, where Leo was waiting with the truck engine running.

"Get in!" he urged.

They scrambled into the vehicle as guards shouting grew louder behind them.

William floored the accelerator, the truck lurching forward as police sirens wailed in the distance.

Navigating through the maze of streets, William evaded pursuit, avoiding main roads and highways. The noise of the sirens eventually faded into the background.

"Safe for now," William muttered, his knuckles white on the steering wheel.

Jonathan and James exchanged weary glances, their faces pale but relieved.

"Well, we didn't get the painting," Jonathan quipped, "but that was more intense than any action movie I've ever seen."

James sighed, "I had a nightmare about this earlier. Let's hope that's the end of it."

William glanced back, his tone measured but stern, "We're lucky to be free. Focus on what's next—we're not out of the woods yet."

The truck slowed to a stop outside Lisha's apartment building. The sky was still shrouded in a hazy gray-black, but the early morning traffic in downtown Manhattan was already beginning to stir.

Inside the vehicle, silence lingered as they braced themselves for what was to come. The mission had failed, but the consequences were only just beginning.

Chapter X. **A Big Blow Up**

Media Frenzy

Morning sunlight bathed the streets of Manhattan, but the atmosphere inside the museum was thick with tension. Police sirens wailed outside as officers moved purposefully, their footsteps echoing through the halls. Flashing red and blue lights caught the attention of curious passersby while headlines dominated the city's morning news: "Foiled Heist Shocks New York-Was the Target Marilyn Monroe's Portrait?"

Around 6 a.m., the museum director and several senior staff members rushed to the scene. They gathered in the surveillance room, glued to the looping security footage. On-screen, a few shadowy figures moved swiftly, their faces obscured by masks, making identification impossible.

"They seemed to know how to avoid most of the infrared sensors and cameras," a technician explained, "but a signal from one of the infrared alarms was triggered, which set off the main alert, forcing them to abandon their plan."

After thoroughly inspecting the exhibition hall, the police confirmed that the painting *The Last Marilyn Monroe* remained intact, though slightly displaced. The director let out a sigh of relief, but unease lingered in his heart.

One detective spoke quietly to the director. "This group was well-prepared, but we have no evidence suggesting insider involvement. We'll continue investigating and update you as soon as possible."

Meanwhile, the city's newspapers splashed the story across their front pages, each with bold headlines and striking images of the museum:

New York Post: "*Midnight Mayhem: Failed Heist Turns Marilyn Monroe Painting Into a Legend*"

Art Review: "*Who's Eyeing Mailyn Monroe's Secrets?*"

Metro Times: "*The Allure of Art: Why Was the Mailyn Monroe Painting Targeted?*"

The New York Post article was incredibly sensational, vividly recounting the attempted heist and the recent frenzy surrounding the painting. It stated: "This failed theft has only heightened the mystique of *The Last Marilyn Monroe*. Though the heist didn't succeed, it has sent shockwaves through the art world. This is no longer just a painting—it's now a legend."

The story spread like wildfire, drawing throngs of art enthusiasts and curious citizens to the museum. By midday, long lines had formed outside as people clamored to see the painting that narrowly escaped theft.

Inside the gallery, the crowd surged. *The Last Marilyn Monroe* became the undisputed centerpiece, with every visitor pausing before it as if trying to uncover its secrets.

"Look at her eyes," a young visitor murmured. "There's so much emotion she's seeing right through us."

"Did you hear?" another chimed in excitedly. "Someone tried to steal it. Doesn't that mean it's worth a fortune?"

Nearby, a middle-aged couple debated. "No," the husband said, "this painting's value isn't about money. It's about the story and emotion behind it."

Walking on Eggshells

Lisha, William, Jonathan, and James were on edge the entire day, their nerves stretched taut. After work, they all gathered in Lisha's apartment, their eyes glued to the TV as the news continued covering the failed museum heist.

"The operation failed," Jonathan finally broke the silence, his voice heavy with frustration. "I should have thought of it—once a painting enters the museum, it's always fitted with tracking sensors."

"What worries me is that we might have been caught on camera,"

James murmured, anxiety evident in his tone. "Even though we wore masks, with today's technology, it's only a matter of time before they identify us."

Leo, always the rational one, analyzed the footage calmly. "The footage is blurry; you were all wearing masks and gloves. It's unlikely your identities will be exposed."

Though rattled, Jonathan and James had no choice but to return to work at the museum daily, keeping tabs on the unfolding investigation. The museum soon issued a notice requesting all departments to submit reports on *The Last Marilyn Monroe*, hoping to trace its origins.

"This painting not being in the museum's collection records might work in our favor," Jonathan remarked to James. "Without any official record, the museum can't definitively prove it owns the painting, let alone claim it was an attempted theft. Even if we're exposed, they won't be able to accuse us of stealing."

Jonathan and James reported separately to their superiors, confirming that their respective departments had no record of the painting. Maintaining a professional demeanor, Jonathan added, "It's likely an unregistered temporary loan piece." James nodded in agreement and quietly added, "We'll need further investigation, but as of now, it doesn't appear to be part of our collection."

A few days later, feedback from other departments corroborated their statements. The painting wasn't listed in any official museum records. The higher-ups were left baffled: How did the painting end up on display if it didn't belong to the museum? And why was it targeted for theft? The internal investigation hit a dead end.

Meanwhile, the media frenzy surrounding the painting showed no signs of dying down. Some investigative journalists uncovered information about the artist and eventually found a way to contact the old master. Despite their persistence, he refused all interview requests, replying tersely, "Everything I wish to say is already expressed in my work."

Under mounting public pressure, The old master finally agreed to a phone interview with a prominent news station. Speaking with a calm yet resolute tone, he stated, "This painting was sold at a nonprofit gallery in Brooklyn that supports artists. As for the rest, I know nothing. Why did I create this painting? It came from a place deep within me. Marilyn Monroe stirred something inside me I needed to express."

The old master's words sparked widespread discussions about the essence of art. While his story and work deeply moved some, others speculated that it might all be a calculated publicity stunt. Regardless, the interview only deepened the public's fascination with *The Last Marilyn Monroe*, drawing even larger crowds to the museum.

A few days later, the police held a press conference to officially announce that they had identified several suspects and to share the latest developments in the case. The room was packed with reporters, and the relentless flash of cameras illuminated the tense atmosphere. All eyes were fixed on the officer standing at the podium.

"Based on surveillance footage from the Metropolitan Museum, we have confirmed the route the suspects followed during the night of the incident." the officer stated confidently, lightly tapping the notebook on the podium. The screen behind him lit up.

Surveillance footage began to play on the screen, showing three figures moving through the museum corridors. Although their faces were obscured by masks, their silhouettes and movements were visible. Every turn they made and every calculated dodge of the cameras was captured in detail. As the video played, murmurs rippled through the journalists' audience.

A television news anchor narrated the footage, saying: "This video vividly outlines the actions of the three suspects within the museum. Although the faces are difficult to identify, the police are utilizing advanced image processing technology to narrow down their identities further. Police believe this was a meticulously planned operation, with the suspects displaying an intimate knowledge of the museum's internal layout. A special task force has been formed, and the investigation is ongoing."

"They're narrowing down the investigation," Jonathan said anxiously. "At this rate, it's only a matter of time before we're exposed."

"What do we do?" Jonathan asked, furrowing his brow as he turned to Lisha.

Lisha remained silent momentarily before speaking resolutely: "I'll come clean to the media and take all the blame."

"Are you insane?" James nearly jumped out of his seat. "You'll ruin yourself!"

"This is my decision," Lisha replied firmly. "I dragged all of you into this, and it's time for me to end it."

Love Through Hardship

The next day, Lisha invited James for a walk along the East River. Williamsburg, nestled on the Brooklyn side of the river, faces Manhattan, separated only by the flowing waters. From the Williamsburg waterfront, one can see Manhattan's magnificent skyline, which becomes even more breathtaking at sunset.

James's apartment was nearby, so the two strolled through the stylish streets, past countless trendy shops, until they reached the East River. Standing on the wooden boardwalk of the pier, they gazed across the water, watching the setting sun bathe the buildings in hues of gold and crimson.

Linking her arm with James's, Lisha said, "I've decided to take responsibility and admit that I'm the mastermind behind this whole thing."

Lisha had been wrestling with this decision for days. Each time she looked at *The Last Marilyn Monroe*, she felt an indescribable force that reminded her of her grandmother Aliza—her passion for art and resilience in life.

Molly had once told Lisha, "Did you know that in her darkest moments after my father committed suicide, she thought about following him? But when she looked at her two young children, her stubbornness won out. She vowed to endure whatever hardships came her way and raise her kids to adulthood."

Lisha had been shocked to learn that Alizahad contemplated such despair.

Molly showed Lisha a fragment of Aliza's writings:

"I met your father. He was the lighthouse in my life, but our marriage was far from easy. The upheavals and changes in our lives weighed heavily on us. After he left, during those seemingly endless cold nights, I would take out the landscape sketches I'd drawn in my youth and think back to our walks through the streets of Shanghai. Those memories were my only solace."

As Lisha read the words, tears welled in her eyes. At that moment, she understood why she had always been drawn to her grandmother's sketches of old Shanghai streets. They held Aliza's most cherished memories, her most unforgettable love. Through her art and words, Aliza's courage shone through—her passion for Shanghai's old streets, her romance with Mr. Mo, and later, her children, who became her anchor in life.

In Lisha's mind, scenes of Aliza's life unfolded like a film reel: the Bund, the changing streets of Shanghai, the passing decades. Though much had transformed, the love and courage Alizaleft behind remained timeless. This realization, crossing the boundaries of time, gave Lisha immense comfort and energy during her moments of doubt. She decided to risk everything and admit that she was the instigator of the incident. She knew confessing to sneaking the painting into the museum could ruin her reputation and career, but continuing to hide the truth weighed even more heavily on her.

A voice echoed in Lisha's mind, "I can't let Jonathan and James live in constant fear anymore. They've already sacrificed too much for this—I can't watch them sink deeper into this mess."

James, startled by her words, exclaimed, "Why would you do this? If this gets out, it'll ruin you!"

Lisha looked at him firmly. "This is my mess, and I won't let you or Jonathan get dragged down because of me." Seeing the worry in James's eyes, she added, "I know what you're afraid of, but I've made my choice—I'm ready to face the consequences."

James stared at Lisha, speechless. He knew he couldn't change her mind, just as he couldn't stop loving her.

He had always thought he could control everything, but now he realized the world was far beyond anyone's control. As the saying goes, when people plan, God laughs. Suddenly, James understood that Lisha had long since thrown his world off balance. Perhaps that was what drew him to her—her courage and determination. He knew once Lisha made a decision, she wouldn't waver. And that was why he loved her.

As the sunset's glow faded and night descended, the buildings across the river began to sparkle with light. Brooklyn was soon enveloped in darkness, while Manhattan remained a dazzling beacon of light.

"I am the Mastermind"

Early the next morning, Molly was still bottomless in sleep when William gently shook her awake.

"What is it?" Molly asked groggily, rubbing her eyes.

"It's Lisha," William said urgently. "She confessed on the news! She admitted to sneaking the painting into the museum and attempting to retrieve it. She said her only goal was to show the museum and the public a genuine masterpiece that could evoke beauty and profound emotions."

Molly instantly snapped awake and rushed to the living room to turn on the television. Sure enough, the screen displayed *The Last Marilyn Monroe* alongside footage of Lisha.

All the major news outlets in New York covered Lisha's statement. In a televised interview, she openly admitted hiring a professional team to smuggle the painting into the museum and later attempt to extract it. She explained that her motivation was to make people reevaluate the actual value of art through this audacious act.

When Lisha's statement was broadcast, it shocked New York's media landscape.

News and social media were flooded with discussions about this "daring escapade in art history." Some hailed her as a "modern-day Robin Hood of art," praising her for challenging the stagnant rules of the art world and giving a voice to overlooked artists. Others strongly criticized her, accusing her of breaking museum regulations and committing a crime.

"She has used a single painting to challenge our definition of art," an art critic said during a live broadcast. "Whether you agree with her or not, her actions have become a phenomenon, forcing us to rethink the meaning and rules of art."

Meanwhile, the museum found itself in a dilemma.

Jonathan and James privately breathed a sigh of relief, knowing that Lisha's admission had taken the heat off them.

"She's taken the fall for us," Jonathan admitted to James in a hushed conversation. "Now, all the focus is on her. We'll come out of this unscathed as long as we stay quiet."

James, however, couldn't find peace of mind. He knew Lisha had stepped forward to protect them, but the thought of her bearing the weight of public scrutiny and legal consequences alone was unbearable. He resolved to come forward if it became necessary.

As the incident gained traction, major art institutions and galleries began to weigh in, pointing to the deeper issues it revealed within the art world: Do the rules truly serve art?

In a television interview, a veteran art scholar remarked, "This event has shown us that art should not be shackled by capital or rigid rules. Lisha's actions remind us that true art belongs to the people— a connection between souls, not something controlled by commercial interests."

However, not everyone viewed the act positively. Critics accused Lisha of orchestrating a calculated stunt. Some speculated that her actions were intended to boost The Old Master's market value, potentially yielding her massive profits.

When questioned about these allegations, Lisha calmly said, "I have no financial motives. The value of this painting lies in the emotions it stirs, not in its price tag. My only wish is for more people to experience true art and rediscover its power."

Lisha also expressed willingness to donate the painting to the museum if they accept it. "As a piece of humanity's spiritual wealth, a great work of art belongs to the public, not private collectors," she said.

Her sincerity won widespread public admiration, causing many to shift their stance. Even some initial critics began to rally behind her, with newfound respect for her bold and selfless actions.

Chapter XI. **Love Is A Choice**

Veterans Take the Lead

At a critical juncture in the unfolding drama, Lisha's partner, Martin, stepped in to take charge.

Martin Lawrence was a successful Wall Street investor and a former vice president at the bank where Lisha had worked. During their time together, Martin recognized Lisha's exceptional talent, sharp intuition for numbers, and remarkable execution skills. Promoting her to manage the company's billion-dollar fund, Martin saw her professional potential and admired her unwavering dedication to her work. Their strong partnership fostered Martin's deep appreciation and trust in Lisha.

Although a practical realist, Martin had a keen eye for recognizing people's strengths. In Lisha, he saw a reflection of his younger self— a relentless spirit unafraid to challenge mediocrity. While Martin often claimed he didn't understand art and didn't invest in it, Lisha's bold actions forced him to rethink its significance. Her willingness to take risks for *The Last Marilyn Monroe*, driven solely by a belief in its artistic value, moved him deeply. He realized that art wasn't just a commodity for trade but a powerful connection between human souls. Lisha's conviction demonstrated the actual value of art—something beyond market rules—and inspired Martin to support her cause.

Martin was a man of considerable influence in New York, with extensive investments and a broad network of connections. Over the years, his business ventures secured him positions on several boards, including the museum board. Reaching out to the museum's chairman, Martin proposed a solution that could lead to a win-win resolution for all parties involved. The chairman convened a board meeting to discuss Martin's proposal. Understanding the importance of avoiding unnecessary escalation, the board agreed to let the chairman and their legal counsel negotiate with Martin.

One Manhattan morning, Martin met with the museum board members and their legal team in a tense and formal setting.

"This painting is not part of your collection," Martin began bluntly, calm but assertive. "Here is a complete purchase record proving it is Lisha's legally acquired private property. Her actions may have been unorthodox, but they were not criminal."

The legal counsel examined the documents, frowning. "She placed an artwork in the museum without authorization, violating museum protocols. It challenges the integrity of our legal and institutional framework."

Martin smiled slightly. "It's also a call to reevaluate the essence of art. The public's reaction has already proven this painting's impact, bringing unprecedented attention to your museum. Instead of pursuing legal action, why not legitimize this situation by accepting the painting as a donation?"

"A donation?" The counsel raised an eyebrow.

"Yes," Martin said firmly. "Lisha is willing to donate *The Last Marilyn Monroe* to the museum's permanent collection. In return, the museum agrees not to press charges. It would defuse public scrutiny and showcase the museum's openness and inclusivity."

The chairman pondered momentarily, then exchanged quiet words with the counsel before nodding. "This seems to be the best resolution."

The museum soon released an official statement announcing its acceptance of Lisha's donation and clarifying that '*The Last Marilyn Monroe*' was not part of its original collection but rather a unique artistic intervention. The museum acknowledged the painting's significance and agreed to display it permanently.

As Lisha's lawyer, William Gold finalized the donation agreement with the museum. The document ensured that the museum would not pursue legal action against her and would continue to exhibit the painting as part of its collection.

The announcement sparked an even greater sensation. For the first time, the prestigious museum accepted a donation from a private collector who was not a celebrity, marking a historic moment that resonated with the public. Praise poured in for the museum's progressive stance, and media outlets detailed the saga.

James, overwhelmed with excitement, hugged Lisha tightly. "You did it! You've changed the rules and reshaped the future of art."

Lisha smiled softly, gazing out at the dazzling Manhattan skyline. For the first time, she felt an unparalleled sense of fulfillment. She knew this was a victory shared by everyone who truly loved art.

With the museum's statement, the media frenzy intensified. Newspapers, television networks, and online platforms covered every angle of the story—from Lisha's motivations and the painting's history to the museum's response. Every detail became a focal point of public discussion, cementing *The Last Marilyn Monroe* as a modern masterpiece that bridged art, courage, and societal reflection.

An Art Report

The next day, Julia seized the opportunity to write a detailed and thought-provoking report. Her article began by recounting Lisha's reasons for purchasing *The Last Marilyn Monroe* and followed with the bold, controversial story of how she smuggled the painting into the museum. Julia delved into the philosophical questions behind the incident: Who defines the value of art?

"This wasn't merely a challenge to the rules of art," Julia wrote. "It was an experiment in belief and courage. *The Last Marilyn Monroe* is more than just a painting—it's a mirror, reflecting our need to reassess art and its boundaries."

The Art of Defiance: Redefining Boundaries with The Last Marilyn Monroe
By Julia Walton

NEW YORK − In a city synonymous with artistic innovation and breaking boundaries, the story of *The Last Marilyn Monroe* has taken on a life of its own. This enigmatic painting has sparked heated debates and a cultural reckoning within the art world, questioning the systems that define value, creativity, and accessibility in art.

For weeks, visitors have flocked to one of New York's most prestigious museums to witness *The Last Marilyn Monroe*. But the painting's presence in the gallery is anything but conventional—it arrived through a bold and subversive act that now forms part of its legend.

A Defiant Gesture, a Purposeful Message

Lisha, an impassioned art collector and entrepreneur, orchestrated an audacious scheme to bring *The Last Marilyn Monroe* into the museum without official sanction. What she describes as an "act of artistic defiance" aimed to challenge the status quo of the art establishment and highlight art's power to move, provoke, and unite.

"This wasn't about breaking rules for the sake of it," Lisha explained in a televised interview. "It was about showing the world what art can achieve—provoking thought, inspiring connection, and stirring the soul."

Her confession has split opinion. Admirers have compared her to a modern–day Robin Hood of the art world, while critics accuse her of undermining institutional integrity. Regardless of perspective, her actions have reignited a perennial question: Who decides the value of art, and who has the right to experience it?

A Fragmented Icon

At the center of this storm is a painting as intricate and layered as the narrative surrounding it. Created by the reclusive artist known simply as "The Old Master," *The Last Marilyn Monroe* combines the disciplined strokes of Chinese calligraphy with the vibrant depth of Western oil painting. Each textured cube of color contributes to a fractured yet cohesive portrait of Marilyn Monroe, capturing her mythic allure and private vulnerability.

"It's not just a portrait," said one art critic. "It mediates fame, fragility, and the human condition. It invites viewers to see beyond the surface, both of Mailyn Monroe's image and the cultural machinery that shaped it."

The Old Master, famously elusive, offered little commentary in a rare radio interview. "I paint what moves me," he said. "This work reflects what Mailyn Monroe's story awakened in me—a kaleidoscope of beauty, sorrow, and strength."

Personal Legacy, Universal Resonance

For Lisha, *The Last Marilyn Monroe* transcends its status as a masterpiece; it's a deeply personal tribute. The painting resonates with the story of her grandmother, Aliza, a Jewish immigrant who escaped Russia's turmoil for the refuge of 1930s Shanghai. Aliza's life, a mix of resilience and displacement, parallels Mailyn Monroe's external radiance and internal struggles.

"Art connects us across time and space," Lisha reflected. "Through this painting, I found a way to honor my grandmother's legacy while grappling with themes of identity and endurance."

Breaking the Rules to Reshape Them

Initially introduced to the public through unsanctioned means, *The Last Marilyn Monroe* has since been formally embraced by the museum. Its controversial entry has challenged the traditional gatekeeping mechanisms of the art world and posed critical questions about how value is determined.

"Lisha's act forces us to confront whether institutions serve the public or the market," noted an art historian during a recent panel discussion. "It's a pivotal moment, underscoring the need for a more inclusive and democratized art world."

By bringing *The Last Marilyn Monroe* to light, Lisha

also amplified the voice of The Old Master, a relatively unknown artist whose groundbreaking fusion of Eastern and Western techniques is now being widely celebrated.

A Cultural Phenomenon

What began as a rebellious gesture has become a cultural touchstone. *The Last Marilyn Monroe* is no longer just a painting—it's a movement, a symbol of art's power to transcend barriers and ignite dialogue.

"Art belongs to everyone," Lisha declared in a final interview. "It's not about who owns or displays it—it's about who sees it, who feels it, and who is changed by it."

As twilight settles over New York, the museum remains alive with the hum of visitors, each drawn to the painting's magnetic pull. Mailyn Monroe's fragmented visage, pieced together through cubes of vibrant color, serves as a reminder: art's greatest power lies not in adhering to rules but in challenging them.

Julia's report ultimately became a pivotal chapter in the legend of *The Last Marilyn Monroe*, adding a thought-provoking punctuation mark to the art world's whirlwind controversy.

Upon publication, her deeply emotional piece garnered widespread acclaim from readers. One commented, "For the first time, I feel like a painting can carry so many stories, making history feel within reach." Another wrote, "Julia revealed the profound intersection of art and humanity—I was deeply moved."

While her article received praise, it also sparked significant controversy. Many hailed Julia for delivering a "wake-up call" to the art world, applauding her for subtly exposing the absurdities of the art market and addressing the essence of art itself.

However, not everyone was convinced. In an interview, a prominent art critic remarked, "The value of art is inherently diverse. Both are integral to the artistic, shaped by market rules or individual pursuit. Julia's article, while passionate, seems overly one-sided, glorifying a single painter, painting, and collector, while neglecting art's complexity and raising questions about her objectivity."

Some even questioned Julia's motivations, accusing her of using the piece to stir controversy and boost her influence. Radical voices labeled her an "attention-seeking writer" who had strayed from the impartiality expected of an art journalist.

As the debates intensified, Julia found herself under intense public scrutiny. While gratified by her article's widespread impact, she also felt unprecedented pressure.

During dinner at their favorite Manhattan restaurant, Julia sighed to Jonathan, "I bet my latest article has ruffled quite a few feathers. Who knows? They might end up replacing me as the columnist."

Jonathan could sense the immense pressure Julia was under, and it made his heart ache. Julia was the most important person in his life—the one who had helped him find direction during his most lost years, giving him a safe harbor and the warmth of love. There was a time when he rebelled against art, refusing to take over his parents' gallery and escaping to France for several years. Even applying to Yale was a means to flee from a suffocating relationship he had in France. But then he met Julia. Her genuine insights into art drew him in, and for the first time, he felt understood, no longer a solitary wanderer in spirit. Once a drifter who had lost faith in marriage, Jonathan now held a prestigious position at one of the world's leading museums, with a soulmate as his life partner. Without Julia, there would be no Jonathan as he was today.

In this moment, as Julia faced her setbacks, Jonathan knew he had to be her anchor, just as she had been his. He needed to support her in pursuing what truly mattered: to fulfill her calling.

Jonathan took her hand and said, "If that's the case, maybe it's for the best. Why don't you just quit and come home? Write a book. Capture everything you want to say about art."

"A book?" Julia asked, surprised.

Jonathan nodded, his grip on her hand tightening. "We've saved enough. It'll cover you for a year or two. When the book is out, readers will finally understand all your thoughts on art."

Julia fell into thoughtful silence, and then her eyes lit up. "You might be right! I should write a book—not just for myself, but for everyone who still believes in art."

Overcome with excitement, she squeezed Jonathan's hand. At that moment, she realized what her true purpose was.

In the bustling restaurant, the surrounding clamor seemed to fade into the background. The couple sat across the table, holding hands tightly, gazing at each other with a love that transported them back to the joy of their early days of courtship and romance.

The Celebration

In Lisha's apartment, everyone gathered to celebrate the successful resolution of the recent events.

The living room table was laden with wine and champagne. Raising her glass, Lisha addressed her friends: "We've done something unforgettable for the sake of art that transcends fame and fortune. For that, I thank you all."

James, Jonathan, Julia, Lee and his wife, Molly, William, and Leo raised their glasses to celebrate.

Jonathan exclaimed, "Oh my God, this has to be the most ridiculous yet meaningful thing I've ever done!"

James laughed, "Even though we technically failed, the outcome exceeded all our expectations. Big thanks to my buddy Jonathan and William—I probably would've been caught that night without you two."

William sipped wine and joked, "I swear I'll never rely on amateurs again—falling short at the critical moment!"

Lee joked, "Well, that's what happens when you don't call me—maybe we would steal it successfully if I were there!"

Molly interjected, "Hey, don't call it stealing—we were reclaiming what was already ours! Lisha paid nearly two hundred grand for that painting. Donating it to the museum? That's way too generous!"

Lee gasped, "Two hundred grand? That's more than a few years of my salary!"

Lisha smiled, "It's not about the money. The museum's acceptance of the painting made my dream come true. One of my lifelong goals was to donate a painting to the Metropolitan Museum of Art. Now that dream is realized, onto the next!"

Martin, who had been quietly observing, added, "The museum offered to pay Lisha for the painting, but she refused. She wanted it to be a formal donation!"

Everyone gasped in admiration, and Julia raised her glass with a laugh. "Alright, let's toast Lisha's generosity and the perfect conclusion of this incredible adventure!"

Jonathan nodded and turned to Leo, lifting his glass, "We also owe this to Leo. We wouldn't have made it out that night without his tech wizardry."

Slightly tipsy, Leo waved them off, "You should thank William. I only did this because of him."

Jonathan smiled and said, "I joined this madness for one reason only: I was moved by James's love for Lisha."

He shot James a meaningful look, and James, understanding, set down his glass and walked over to Lisha. "Darling," he began, "I would walk through fire for you."

The room erupted into cheers as everyone clinked their glasses, encouraging the couple to share a kiss. James swept Lisha off her feet, twirled her around, and then placed her back down, pulling her into a deep embrace.

As the room filled with laughter and applause, a soft guitar melody began to play. Molly had planned, slipping on a record she had purchased from the street musician they admired.

Suddenly, James knelt on one knee before Lisha and said, "Lisha, you are the love of my life. I knew we were destined to be together from the moment I first saw you. I want to spend the rest of my life with you. Would you marry me?"

It was James's second proposal to Lisha. The room fell silent, all eyes on her as they awaited her answer.

Lisha looked down at James, her emotions swirling. She had known him for over a year but had never imagined he could be her future. When he had proposed a month ago, she had found it amusing. Now, her perspective had changed entirely. What was there to wait for if a man was willing to walk through fire for her?

She bent down slightly and said softly, "Our destiny has arrived. Yes, I will."

James leaped to his feet, embraced Lisha tightly, and kissed her again, this time with tears of joy.

Lisha smiled through happy tears, "You should thank *The Last Marilyn Monroe*. It's the reason we're here together today."

The room filled with congratulations and joy as everyone celebrated the couple's love.

Through the windows, Manhattan's skyline shimmered in neon lights against the night sky, glowing with a beauty that felt just right for the moment.

A Family Tale

On their drive back to Long Island, William and Molly listened to the soothing guitar melodies of the street musician as they chatted about *The Last Marilyn Monroe*.

William spoke in a tone of sincere admiration, "Molly, I have to say, Lisha truly isn't in this for fame or fortune. She's completely dedicated to art. I'm genuinely impressed. I was upset initially, thinking she dragged everyone into this risky situation over an unrelated artist and a painting."

Molly teased, "Well, you've always known my niece loves to shake things up. And now you're impressed by her, huh?"

William said apologetically, "I used to think the art market wasn't as pure as you all imagined. When a painting becomes a sensation, people sing its praises and admire the courage and vision behind it. But when the tide turns, it can suddenly become a target for criticism. I've always believed the market doesn't care about truth, only trends. But now, I realize Lisha's actions reshaped the market and created a new trend!"

Molly said gently, "I never expected this—you might not understand at first, but once you do, you see it clearer than anyone else."

William's energy surged, "What Lisha did inspired me. You need to seize this moment and get your book out there. The story you're writing about Aliza 's family will be big!"

Molly smiled, "Aliza and Mailyn Monroe are connected in some way. When Aliza was 18, she looked strikingly similar to *The Last Marilyn Monroe*. It's not just her appearance—it's that subtle melancholy beneath her charm. It's like it was born with her."

William nodded thoughtfully. "Hearing you say that, it sounds incredible. You should get home and finish writing. I can already picture someone turning your book into a movie someday."

Molly gazed out at the night sky for a moment, silent. Then she quietly turned to look at William's focused profile as he drove. A warm sense of gratitude welled up in her heart. "Thank you, love," she said softly. "Thank you for supporting me. Without you, I don't think I'd have the strength to keep writing this book."

William reached over and gently squeezed her hand, his voice resolute. "Molly, never doubt yourself. The story you're telling will touch people's hearts."

The car fell quiet again, leaving only the flowing melodies of the guitar playing through the speakers. Accompanied by this shared moment of understanding and anticipation, the car glided smoothly along the road into the night.

Chapter XII. **The Seasons of Harvest**

Spring in New York

The Old Master's Studio

The sunlight poured over the stone steps in front of the Metropolitan Museum while a gentle spring breeze brushed against the faces of visitors. The air was filled with the vitality and freshness of spring. A street musician, cradling an electric guitar, played soft and enchanting melodies, adding a touch of warmth and serenity to the bustling crowd.

Inside the museum, crowds gathered around a single painting, their phones clicking in unison. The artwork in question, The Last Marilyn, once sparked widespread controversy but now hung proudly in the central gallery, the indisputable focus of attention.

Despite the media frenzy surrounding the piece, the artist remained elusive, refusing all interview requests. The only exception was his decision to accept Lisha as his agent and entrust her with organizing his future exhibitions. To him, Lisha understood his inner world and could convey his artistic philosophy to a broader audience.

Lisha finally visited the artist's studio in upstate New York, nestled at the foot of the Catskill Mountains. The estate's design drew inspiration from a European aristocratic aesthetic, exuding a rich sense of history and regional character. Surrounded by expansive forests and picturesque hills, the studio seemed to merge seamlessly with its natural surroundings, as if it had grown organically from the land.

The studio's exterior was a Federal-style building with red brick walls and white colonnades, radiating the charm of 19th-century architecture. Its steeply pitched roof blended with the misty mountain landscape, while a cobblestone path flanked by native wildflowers, which changed colors with the seasons, led to the entrance.

Inside, the studio was spacious and filled with natural light, reflecting the practical yet aesthetic sensibilities of New England architecture. The central hall, an open creative space, featured polished wooden floors harmonizing with the surrounding environment. Exposed wooden beams added a rustic charm to the high ceilings.

A massive wooden easel stood as the centerpiece by a floor-to-ceiling window, commanding attention within the studio. Through the glass, the view extended to dense forests and rolling hills. Sunlight streamed in, casting a soft, dreamlike glow across the room. Along the windowed wall stood custom white wooden shelves neatly lined with tubes of paint. The vibrant array resembled an ocean of colors, leaving Lisha in awe. Recognizing the premium quality of the European oil paints, she couldn't help but gasp. Growing up watching her father paint, she knew the cost of such materials well. Even during her time at art academy, she had hesitated before splurging on expensive paints—but here was a meticulously organized treasure trove of them.

The walls were adorned with paintings, their vivid colors and textured brushstrokes creating a stunning visual impact. Near the windows hung a few of the artist's early abstract works from his New York days, brimming with urban tension and emotional conflict. However, the majority were recent creations—grand, almost pulsating with the energy of nature and the passage of time. Lisha gazed at each piece as though wandering through a private museum.

At that moment, she understood why the artist had chosen a life of reclusion. This studio was more than a workspace; it was a sanctuary where he could converse with his art and delve into self-discovery. It was a refuge, shielded from the world's noise and chaos, enveloped in the serenity of nature.

Her gaze landed on the artist's early works, drawn by an invisible force. The colors on the canvas clashed and harmonized, reflecting the inspiration and tension of New York City while hinting at a deep nostalgia for his Jiangnan homeland. These paintings depicted idyllic waterways and poetic landscapes juxtaposed with Western symbols like Eve, apples, and devils—an interplay of temptation and conflict. The narratives on the canvas transcended cultures and eras, weaving a story both familiar and enigmatic. Lisha felt like she had entered a wordless dream where culture and emotion resonated deeply. The power of the paintings lay not only in their technique but also in the artist's profound understanding of two distinct worlds.

Reflecting on these works, Lisha recalled the artist's words: "These paintings have tension, but they carry too many shadows of others. If I continued down this path, I might achieve success, but it wouldn't be my success. These works lack my soul. They tread a well-worn road, but art should be about forging your own path. Even if it's lonely and untraveled, it must be walked. Life should stand out, not be wasted in mediocrity."

As she pondered his words, Lisha thought of her grandfather, Mr. Mo. In an era of political turmoil and oppression, many chose endurance, living humble lives like ants. Yet Mr. Mo chose another path. His actions were deemed severing ties with the party and the people, but Lisha saw them as acts of defiance—a refusal to compromise his identity. She couldn't help but wonder: Did the artist and her grandfather share a similar spirit? One resisted through his life; the other through his art. Both, in their ways, sought authenticity.

Lisha's mind whirled. Their choices came at a profound cost: her grandfather paid with his life, while the artist sacrificed solitude and time for independence and artistic transcendence. She realized she could do nothing to change her grandfather's fate, but she could support the artist's vision. Perhaps that's why she had risked so much for The Last Marilyn. It wasn't just about the painting but about answering a call from deep within—a pursuit of freedom across time and existence.

The studio was steeped in history and creativity. In one corner stood a vintage wooden desk with Chinese calligraphy tools, suggesting the artist's daily practice. At the center, an old fireplace added warmth to the space, above which a ticking bronze clock seemed to mark the passage of time.

Outside the studio, a small courtyard led to dense woods. Towering oaks and lavender bushes filled the air with earthy and floral scents. Lisha imagined the artist sitting on a bench in the courtyard, sipping tea, gazing at the distant mountains, and losing himself in thought.

This studio was a creative space and a temple of art and soul, blending tradition and individuality. Every detail told its owner's story—a convergence of inspiration and nature.

As Lisha examined the bookshelves, she stumbled upon old photos: snapshots of the artist in his youth and records of his children growing from infants to adults. In one image, the artist stands on stage, electric guitar in hand, long hair flying under dazzling lights. In another, he hosts a TV show brimming with youthful confidence and audacity. The images stunned Lisha, who suddenly realizes the artist is of the same generation as her aunt Molly.

Through these photos, Lisha pieced together a timeline spanning continents and decades: the artist arrived in New York slightly earlier than Molly but later traveled across Taiwan, Singapore, Beijing, and Shanghai before returning to New York to embark on a new artistic journey. On the other hand, Molly came to New York in her twenties, starting from scratch and carving her challenging path.

Lisha reflected on their shared generational experience living through China's most turbulent transformations. As witnesses to the Cultural Revolution's devastation and the reform era's economic rise, they bore the weight of destruction and renewal. Now settled in New York, they found a "second home" where they could redefine themselves.

Standing before the bookshelves, Lisha felt a deep connection to their resilience and determination—a testament to their unwavering pursuit of freedom and expression. This connection seemed to bridge time and space, linking her life to theirs in profound and mysterious ways.

Art Fund

Lisha finally realized her dream of establishing her art fund and formally entering the field of art investment and management. This fund became an extension of her artistic vision and the foundation of a brand-new career.

Martin was her first major shareholder, leveraging his extensive Wall Street connections and investment expertise to provide substantial financial support. He was not only an investment partner but also a crucial driving force behind Lisha's burgeoning career. With his help, the fund quickly drew the attention of numerous potential clients and art institutions.

Molly and William Gold, early supporters, eagerly joined the ranks of investors. They were both family and dedicated advocates of the fund. William, ever the humorist, quipped to Lisha and Molly, "Since you both have such a passion for genuinely valuable art, my little private detective agency might as well throw in some capital to help you turn art into big business."

James, too, joined the fund with a unique enthusiasm. He wanted to support Lisha's career through concrete actions and hoped this shared endeavor would deepen their emotional bond. Teasingly, he told her, "This is the most serious investment I've ever made—not just in art but in you."

With the backing of her supporters, Lisha's art fund quickly gained prominence. Every time the fund's exhibitions, auctions, and fundraising galas achieved success, Lisha would stand in the spotlight, addressing the applause with heartfelt sincerity:

"This art fund belongs to everyone who loves art and believes in the power of creativity. It is your support that keeps art alive and dreams achievable."

Her authenticity and conviction resonated with everyone in the room, leaving them inspired by the pure sense of purpose and boundless possibilities that the fund represented.

Winning Her Heart

On a spring evening, as night descended, the serene stillness of the Metropolitan Museum of Art after closing hours enveloped the gallery. Amid the quiet, *The Last Marilyn Monroe* glowed softly under the lights. James held Lisha's hand as he guided her toward the painting.

"James, I know why you brought me here!" Lisha said with a laugh. "Last time we were here after hours for a private viewing, I told Jonathan that *The Last Marilyn Monroe* deserved to be displayed at the MET for everyone to see. And now, here it is!"

James smiled at her, his gaze filled with warmth. "I remember you said, 'When the time is right,' and I didn't fully understand then. But now, I do."

"And what do you mean by that?" Lisha asked playfully, her sparkling eyes reflecting the painting's glow.

James gave a mysterious smile and gently turned her to face *The Last Marilyn Monroe*. His expression radiated deep affection as though he wished to etch every detail of the moment into their shared memory.

Suddenly, the gallery lights brightened, and familiar faces emerged—friends, reporters, and MET staff—holding flowers, cakes, and balloons, all beaming as they approached.

Before Lisha could fully process her surprise, soft music began to play. James knelt on one knee, a diamond ring glinting in his hand. He looked at her with unwavering devotion and said, "Lisha, you are the love of my life. Will you marry me?"

Tears of joy sparkled in Lisha's eyes as she answered without hesitation, "Yes, I will."

Cheers and applause filled the gallery as the couple embraced tightly. James had fulfilled his dream—proposing to the woman he loved in front of *The Last Marilyn Monroe*, creating a moment as unforgettable as the masterpiece itself.

Outside the MET, the spring breeze swept through Manhattan's glittering streets, carrying the faint fragrance of blooming flowers, a perfect prelude to a new chapter in their lives.

Summer in New York

Molly's Wedding

In the most beautiful summer in New York, Molly and William Gold held their wedding in a sunlit garden on Long Island, surrounded by all their friends who came to celebrate. Under the radiant sunlight, colorful balloons swayed gently in the breeze, accompanied by the melodic strains of a violin. The wedding aisle was adorned with a carpet of blush pink and champagne-colored petals.

As one of William's groomsmen, James stood alongside Leo, watching Professor Li, Lisha's father, escorted Molly down the aisle.

To attend Molly's second wedding, Professor Li and his wife, Mo Hua, had flown to New York. Both were overjoyed and elegantly dressed for the occasion.

At the pre-wedding celebration, Molly recounted the legendary story of The Last Marilyn. Her sister, Mo Hua and brother-in-law, Professor Li, listened in astonishment and deep emotion. This bizarre and almost unbelievable artistic adventure made them feel as if they were living in a modern-day Arabian Nights tale.

Molly spoke with heartfelt gratitude: "If it weren't for William, Lisha's dream could never have come true. The world might never have known about the old master's work. Most importantly, I wouldn't have completed the biography of Aliza's family. *The Last Marilyn Monroe* is not just a painting; it's a catalyst. It connected our destinies and made me realize that William is my soulmate."

She continued, "William's actions showed me that people with high energy instinctively help others achieve their dreams. He has made me a better person and convinced me that my dreams are meaningful and my stories worth telling. He is the one who makes me feel supported and understood."

Professor Li, deeply moved, responded, "This is truly touching. It is the spirit of art at its finest. The power of art lies in its ability to inspire others and help them reach greater heights. This belief and action embody the ultimate purpose of art's existence."

Mo Hua added with emotion, "Perhaps stories like this can only happen in New York. After all, the Metropolitan Museum of Art was founded to promote art education and guide the public. Through your efforts, this museum has again demonstrated why it is a world-class institution, reminding everyone of art's power and value."

At the wedding, Lisha, one of Molly's bridesmaids, looked exceptionally stunning. She and Julia, the other bridesmaid, wore elegant blush-colored gowns and stood beside Molly, who held a bouquet of champagne and pink roses.

Under the photographer's lens, Molly, dressed in an ivory wedding gown, gazed lovingly at William, who wore a gray suit with a boutonniere of two-tone roses pinned to his lapel. With the pastor's blessing, the couple sealed their vows with a romantic kiss, officially becoming husband and wife.

When Molly turned her back to the guests and tossed her bouquet, it arced gracefully through the air and landed right in front of Lisha. Quick as a flash, James caught it and handed it to her with a smile. "It seems destiny has spoken," he said. Lisha couldn't help but laugh and gave him a gentle nod.

Amid cheers and laughter, Molly and William shared their first dance, followed by Professor Li and his wife, James and Lisha, Jonathan and Julia, the Lee couple, and other guests who joined in the joyous celebration.

It was a scene of pure joy and celebration, forever etched into the memories of everyone present.

The Best Seller

Summer had arrived on Manhattan Island, painting the city in vibrant greens and blooming flowers. In a bright and spacious bookstore downtown, stacks of bestsellers adorned the tables, and prominently displayed at the center was *The Last Marilyn Monroe*, Julia's latest novel. The book, written in a literary style, narrated how the painting had been stealthily brought into and almost taken out of the Metropolitan Museum of Art, weaving in the tales of all the key players involved.

At the launch and signing event, a long line stretched out in front of the bookstore, with fans eagerly waiting for Julia's autograph. Among them were Professor Li, his wife, Lisha, Molly, and other friends, slowly making their way forward in the queue.

Jonathan chuckled, saying, "Julia already set aside copies for you all. You didn't have to wait in line." Molly smiled and replied, "We're here to show support—and to witness her hard work and success."

Professor Li turned to Lisha and said, "The story of *The Last Marilyn Monroe* has deeply moved me. I've decided to stay in New York and work with your art foundation. Let's bring more talented artists like the old master into your circle. Who knows, one day, we might even establish a contemporary art museum here."

Mo Hua sighed and said, "Like father, like daughter indeed."

Just then, a uniquely melodic guitar tune began to flow like water through the air. Lisha immediately perked up, scanning the surroundings. Jonathan grinned and said, "I invited the musician to play a few pieces for the crowd." Lisha turned toward the bookstore entrance, and sure enough, there was the familiar guitarist who often played outside the Metropolitan Museum of Art, now seated near the door, strumming his beautiful melodies. The gentle sound of the music flowed into the ears and hearts of passersby.

Lisha paused, lost in thought. In her mind's eye, the image of *The Last Marilyn Monroe* appeared vividly—each brushstroke and color cube stood out in sharp clarity. As the vision shifted to the painting's composition, its harmony became even more apparent. Suddenly, inspiration struck her.

Autumn in New York

A Solo Exhibition

Autumn in New York, the city's most beautiful season, painted Manhattan with golden and fiery red leaves. In a renowned downtown art gallery, the warm glow of lights illuminated a buzzing opening night filled with the clinking of glasses and lively conversation.

The gallery walls showcased a collection of vibrant paintings. From a distance, they appeared as realistic depictions of landscapes and portraits, but up close, the canvases revealed a kaleidoscope of oil paint strokes formed from calligraphy-like cubes. It was the solo exhibition of the reclusive old master, organized by Lisha.

Gentle strains of an Eastern-inspired guitar solo filled the exhibition space, creating a serene ambiance that harmonized perfectly with the artwork on the walls.

At the gallery entrance, a white wooden board adorned with bananas drew a small crowd. Next to it stood a handwritten sign: "25 cents each, $1 for four."

A few visitors chuckled at the display.

"Is this performance art?" a young man asked, puzzled.

One attendee pulled out a five-dollar bill, offering to treat everyone to bananas, sparking laughter as the group began eating and chatting.

"I think it's mocking that guy who bought a banana for $6.8 million," another visitor said, shaking their head. "It's a satire about the absurdity of the art market. Honestly, this pricing feels right. Art is wonderful, but those so-called works that blatantly insult our intelligence are just infuriating."

"Exactly!" chimed in a stylish young woman. "Selling a banana for $6.8 million is insane. The buyer even wanted Elon Musk to send it to space, but Musk refused. These people are nuts!"

"Is there a difference between crazy people and artists?" a young man teased.

"Of course, there is!" the stylish woman retorted. "The difference lies in whether the work has beauty. Art should evoke beauty, not just create publicity stunts."

"Still, the artist and the banana buyer both became famous. From a self-promotion standpoint, wasn't it a success?" another voice interjected.

"But fame should carry positive energy," the woman countered. "True art gains recognition by touching hearts, not through ridiculous gimmicks."

An older attendee nodded in agreement, "Wealth should be earned honorably, and fame is no different. Fame achieved without integrity is neither noble nor respectable, especially when it exploits art."

The group's animated discussion attracted attention, their voices mingling in the lively atmosphere.

Standing nearby, Martin listened with a faint smile. He appreciated their candid opinions and passion, which starkly contrasted with the pretentiousness he had often encountered in art. He remembered feeling alienated at galleries where people stood before artworks, feigning profound understanding by saying, "I can feel the artist's pain." Here, he felt a refreshing authenticity.

Compelled by the crowd's energy, Martin joined the conversation: "Honestly, when I read the Wall Street article about the banana, I felt like I'd swallowed a fly. Art is inherently beautiful—why make it absurd? Art shouldn't require you to 'get it.' You either like it or you don't. That's the real connection, isn't it?"

His words resonated, drawing nods of agreement. Martin felt a rekindled love for art for the first time in years, recalling Lisha's words: "Art is like music—it's not about high or low, just intuition and emotion."

Nearby, Lisha, chatting with the exhibition curator, Tao Hua, overheard the banana discussion and smiled knowingly.

James quietly approached her side and whispered, "This was your idea, wasn't it? Pretty good, I like it!"

Lisha chuckled. "It's a statement. To me, a banana is worth what it costs. True art is what's displayed here." She gestured toward the old master's paintings, her tone resolute.

As the camera pans out, the gallery reveals a juxtaposition of art and bananas, symbolizing a critique of the absurdities of the art market. In the distance, among the guests, a distinguished-looking old artist seemed to be standing near Lisha and Tao Hua. Yet, he disappeared in a flash before the camera could focus on his face. As expected, the old artist wasn't fond of such lively gatherings and quietly slipped away.

Visitors gathered before a striking portrait of a woman prominently displayed on the main wall. The subject was Lisha's grandmother, Aliza, radiating the grace and charm of 1940s Shanghai. The intricate interplay of vibrant oil paint and calligraphy-like strokes gave the piece an almost ethereal quality.

"Who is she?" whispered visitors, captivated by the timeless beauty. Beside the painting, a exhibition lable bore a small red dot, signifying it had already been sold.

Lisha stood across from the portrait of Aliza, her grandmother, gazing through the ebb and flow of the crowd with a heart full of emotion. At long last, her beloved Aliza had been brought back to life as a piece of art, presented once more to the public. The era she lived through, the stories she experienced, and the historical changes she witnessed were subtly etched into the shimmering layers of oil paint and the aura emanating from the figure in the artwork. A hundred years from now, this generation will be gone. Still, the art will endure—preserving the history of a family and the captivating essence of its artistry, much like Klimt's Lady in Gold, leaving an everlasting legacy.

In the gallery's gift shop, a visitor asked the staff, "Who's the musician behind the music playing in the exhibition?"

The young clerk smiled. "I'm not sure, but we're selling his CDs over there if you're interested."

Excitedly, the visitor rushed to purchase a CD.

James approached Lisha and commented, "Amazing. You're pairing the street musician's melodies with the old master's paintings. It's a perfect match—immersive and brilliant."

Lisha smiled, "Music flows freely, carrying its spirit wherever it goes. Painting, on the other hand, requires solitude and contemplation to achieve timelessness."

James grinned, "Don't you think their art complements each other? It feels like they were created for one another—almost like the same artist made both."

Lisha's eyes widened as a thought struck her. She remembered the music she'd heard while visiting the old master's studio, where his paintings adorned the walls and a similar melody filled the air. Could it be more than a coincidence?

Leaning toward James, she whispered her suspicions. As the mystery deepened, his expression shifted from surprise to agreement.

The Book

On the bookshelves of the art shop, a variety of art books were neatly displayed for sale. Among them, one cover stood out in the spotlight: a black-and-white photo of young Aliza, with the title *Dreaming of Shanghai: The Story of a Russian-Jewish Descendant in Shanghai*. The author was Molly. At last, Molly's nonfiction work about Aliza's life was published. The book included family photographs in black and white, Aliza's sketches and watercolors of streets near Avenue Joffre, fragments of her diary, and even photos of a young Molly and a little Lisha. It told a moving tale of love and loss, joy and sorrow, against the backdrop of historical upheavals beyond the control of ordinary people.

A few visitors who had admired the mysterious and captivating 1940s woman depicted in the gallery's portrait now noticed the book and began flipping through its pages, eagerly discussing it.

"Wow, the painting looks just like her," one reader remarked, gesturing toward the old master's portrait.

"I think the painting is extraordinary," another said. "It captured Aliza 's longing and anticipation—maybe even a touch of sadness."

Unable to resist, Lisha pulled Molly forward and introduced her to the group. "We'll soon be organizing a book discussion event where the author can share stories about Aliza 's era with everyone," she said warmly.

The visitors lit up with excitement. "That's wonderful! Please let us know—we'll be there!" they exclaimed, hurrying to the gallery's front desk to leave their names and contact information.

Watching their enthusiastic retreat, Lisha turned to Molly and said, "I never imagined your book would finally bring the real Aliza to light."

Molly smiled wistfully. "Even though my book hasn't become a bestseller like Julia's, getting it written and published was my greatest wish."

Lisha reassured her, "You know as well as I do that great art doesn't need the art world's approval to shine. Your book is the same, though it is a niche for now, and every review is five stars. It'll find its place on the bestseller lists eventually."

Standing nearby, William said, "Lisha, you may not know this, but Molly's book has already been optioned by a Hollywood director who plans to turn it into a feature film. Soon, your aunt will be a celebrity!"

Molly playfully scolded him with a smile: "William, this is Lisha's first solo exhibition for the old master, Don't use this opportunity to sneak in your own agenda."

William feigned innocence, "Side business? What are you talking about?"

Before Molly could respond, Martin eagerly interjected, "Our foundation wants to buy the rights to your book and invest in the movie, too!"

William looked a bit puzzled and asked, "What do you mean by 'sneak in my own agenda'?"

Molly rolled her eyes at the two men, "You two! Always thinking about money. What do you know about literature and art?"

Lisha joyfully hugged Molly, "Congratulations! It looks like our foundation has found another artist to support!"

Turning to Molly, Lisha added, "By the way, I've already picked the music composer for the film—it has to be him."

Molly raised an eyebrow, "You mean the street musician? I agree—his music perfectly matches Aliza's era, with such a strong sense of nostalgia."

As Julia, Jonathan, and James walked over, they overheard Molly's words and exchanged knowing smiles. They all clearly understood the secret Lisha had whispered to James earlier.

The Movie

On a sunny autumn afternoon in New York, friends gathered for a picnic in Brooklyn's East River Park. Across the shimmering water, Manhattan's skyline gleamed like sunlight dancing on ripples. Among them, the street musician Lisha had invited sat in the center, strumming his guitar. The group encircled him, lost in the spell of his soulful melodies.

At that moment, a young stranger approached the group, smiling politely. He turned to Julia and said, "Excuse me, may I interrupt for a moment?"

Julia, curious, looked up and replied, "Of course, you're welcome to join our picnic. We've got plenty of food and drinks."

The young man introduced himself, saying, "I'm the old master's son, just back from filming in Asia. I'm a filmmaker and recently read your book, *The Last Marilyn Monroe*. It moved me deeply. I wanted to share some exciting news: my team plans to adapt your book into our next film."

Everyone froze for a moment, stunned by the serendipity. Lisha raised an eyebrow with a playful smile, "So this movie will tell the story of our own 'thrilling adventure'?"

The young man nodded, a glint of mystery in his eyes. "Not just that. I also want to reveal some details you might not know. My father initially stopped painting for 16 years to earn enough money to give us the best education. During that time, he discovered a new artistic language. In 2001, he returned to art with his new visual language. To me, he's the true master of fine art."

The group was deeply moved, and a wave of discussion swept through.

Julia remarked, "That sounds like the perfect ending for the film."

The young man smiled warmly at Julia and Lisha and added, "Thank you both for supporting and helping my father. "If it weren't for you, my father might never have seen his art finally displayed in the Metropolitan Museum during his lifetime."

James, Jonathan, and William grinned, saying, "And us! What about us!"

The young man chuckled. "Of course, you're all the heroes of my story."

With that, he rose to leave. As he walked toward the street musician, the song concluded. The musician looked up at his son, and on his face was a smile everyone recognized.

Only then did the group realize the truth: the street musician they'd known so well was the old master himself! No wonder his music paired so perfectly with his art.

As the music flowed, the camera slowly pulled back, the crowd listening to the music faded into a blur, while Lisha's close-up gaze gradually came into sharp focus. She turned her eyes away from the father and son duo, raised her glass, and said, "To our shared destiny and our belief in the beauty of art! A year ago, none of us could have imagined this day. Fate has brought us together, helping us all find purpose and direction in our lives."

Jonathan interjected with a grin, "...and love."

Lisha's father raised his glass and said with heartfelt emotion, "Thank you all for supporting and caring for Lisha. She has found a second home here in New York, just as her grandmother Aliza's family once found their second home in Shanghai."

Molly and Mo Hua exchanged a knowing smile. Molly said, "Aliza's story continues in New York. Though she never made it here to reunite with her family, today, through Lisha and the legacy of *The Last Marilyn Monroe*, we're all finally together. It's the power of art that has brought us here."

James laughed, "Finally, let's raise a toast to *The Last Marilyn Monroe*. Without this painting, there wouldn't be the life Lisha and I share today, nor the wild friendship we all now cherish."

Molly laughed, saying, "As the saying goes, fortune favors the bold!" Her remark drew another round of laughter.

Amid the joyous conversation, time seemed to slip away, just like every fleeting day of our lives. Each dawn, dusk, flower, and memory carries its unique story of art, friendship, and love.

Winter in New York

A year later, snow blanketed Manhattan, transforming the city into a winter wonderland filled with holiday cheer. Festive lights and decorations adorned every corner, from the twinkling neon of Times Square to the meticulously styled shop windows. Smiling crowds bustled through the streets, bundled in warm coats, holding steaming cups of coffee, and reveling in the season's magic.

Outside a bustling cinema, people stood in line waiting, chatting excitedly as they braved the cold. Above the entrance, a glowing marquee announced the premiere of The Last Marilyn.

Inside the theater lobby, Lisha, James, Julia, Jonathan, and Molly stood quietly in a corner, observing the eager audience filing into the screening room. Each carried an unspoken mix of joy, nostalgia, and a sense of fulfillment.

"Who would've thought our wild escapade would lead to this?" James broke the silence, his tone tinged with pride.

"Indeed," Lisha replied with a smile. "*The Last Marilyn Monroe* didn't just change our lives—it's shown so many people the true essence of art."

Beaming with pride, Julia added, "I never imagined my book would become a movie. It feels surreal."

At that moment, The old master's son, now an accomplished filmmaker, approached them. With a warm smile, he said, "Thank you all for being here tonight. My father is at home, moved to tears by everything that's happened. True art always finds its rightful stage."

The group nodded, their spirits lifted, and they followed the crowd into the darkened screening room. As the opening music played, they felt transported back to the past year's events, reliving the memories that had brought them to this moment.

After the screening, they stepped out into the snowy night. Lisha looked up at the falling snow, her voice soft as she said to James, "I think my grandmother would be proud of us."

James wrapped his arm around her, smiling. "She absolutely would. And The old master's music will always be with us."

In the distance, city lights shimmered on the snow-covered ground, casting a warm glow on the group's retreating silhouettes. The film's theme song played softly in the background as the camera pulled away, leaving the scene bathed in an enduring sense of hope, art, and connection.

Epilogue

Martin's Art Fund

The scene cut to an office on Wall Street, where Martin passionately addressed a group of investors.

"This wasn't just a painting but an investment in the future. Our foundation would revolutionize contemporary art investment and create an entirely new value chain," he declared confidently.

His phone buzzed, displaying a news notification: "*The Last Marilyn Monroe* became box office number one."

The Street Musician

In the springtime streets of New York, the street musician

strummed a gentle, melodic tune on his guitar. A group of fans suddenly gathered, excitedly snapping photos.

"Oh my gosh! That's the movie soundtrack!" one fan exclaimed.

The musician, surrounded by the crowd, continued playing, unaffected by the commotion. When the song ended, fans clamored for his autograph. He smiled and said wryly, "I'm just a street artist, not a celebrity."

Just then, someone handed him a business card. "We'd love to host a solo concert for you, with the theme Jiangnan."

The Art of Humor

In William's office, he enthusiastically presented a blank white canvas framed elegantly with nothing on it.

"Ladies and gentlemen, this is the centerpiece of our next exhibition: The Void of Art. A painting that contained nothing yet existed, reminding people that the essence of art lay in imagination!" William declared confidently.

Suddenly, his assistant leaned in and whispered, "Boss, this might not be as popular as *The Last Marilyn Monroe*."

William paused, stroking his chin thoughtfully, before replying, "Then let's add a banana."

Everyone burst into laughter. It turned out that William had quite a sense of humor, too.

The Painting

The Last Marilyn Monroe was carefully packed into a specialized shipping crate in the museum's storage room.

"Hey, where's this going?" someone asked.

"Louvre," replied a staff member while sealing the box. "It's replacing Mona Lisa while she undergoes restoration."

"Wow," someone marveled. "That means it's officially one of the most famous paintings in the world now."

Inside the crate, Marilyn's enigmatic smile seemed to hold an air of knowing, as if she had seen through everything the world had to offer.

Julia's New Book

In Julia's study, she typed the final sentence of her latest manuscript.

The title stood boldly at the top: From Marilyn to Eternity: Art, Faith, and Love.

She sighed with relief, lifting her coffee cup to enjoy a moment of peace. Just then, her phone rang. It was her editor.

"Julia, your book has just been picked up for a TV adaptation. Filming starts soon!"

Julia paused in disbelief, then murmured, "It seemed this story had no end."

The Gift

The scene shifted to a sunlit riverside garden, with Manhattan's skyline forming the backdrop. Beneath an arch adorned with blush and ivory roses, Lisha walked down the aisle in an elegant ivory wedding gown, her father by her side. At the altar, James stood tall in a tailored suit, his face glowing with happiness.

Familiar faces flashed among the guests: Julia, Jonathan, William Gold, and Molly. A live band played a memorable melody—the theme song from *The Last Marilyn Monroe*.

As the ceremony reached its joyful peak and guests raised their glasses in celebration, several uniformed movers carried in a large box tied with a golden ribbon, drawing everyone's attention.

The scene faded as the box was set down, leaving the audience wondering what surprises it held.

With James by her side, Lisha slowly untied the satin ribbon. All eyes were on her, even the children standing on tiptoes to catch a glimpse. As the box opened, Lisha froze, her hands covering her mouth, her eyes welling up with tears.

Inside the box was a massive oil painting. Up close, it was a dazzling mosaic of vibrant color cubes, but stepping back revealed an 18-year-old Aliza in a portrait taken in Shanghai—a masterpiece unmistakably created by the old master.

The painting felt so familiar; it was the same one showcased in the old master's solo exhibition the year before.

Molly smiled gently and said, "This is a gift from the old master and us." She gestured to the people behind her: Lisha's parents, William Gold and Molly, and the film director, who represented the old master.

In truth, the old master had sold the painting at a modest price, and Lisha's loved ones had secretly purchased it as a wedding gift for her.

Tears streamed down Lisha's face as she exclaimed, "I saw the red dot last time and knew it had been sold, but I never imagined it was you who bought it, keeping it a secret all this time!"

James smiled and added, "The old master and all of us wanted to give you this surprise to thank you for everything you've done. From now on, this painting will be our family heirloom, witnessing every day of our future together."

At this moment, the scene pulls back, blending the laughter of the guests with the Manhattan skyline. Lisha holds a glass of champagne, gazing into the distance with a serene smile.

AUTHOR'S NOTE

The Last Marilyn Monroe featured in this book is a striking and unconventional oil painting created by the American Chinese artist Stone Chun Shi. The artwork is composed of vibrant, abstract square color cubes, blending abstraction and realism in a way that leaves a lasting impression. Its unique contemporary style aligns perfectly with the novel's plot, serving as the pivotal element in the story of "sneaking the painting into the museum."